Chasin

CHASING

the

DEAD

By Joe Schreiber

CHASING THE DEAD
EAT THE DARK

CHASING

the

DEAD

A NOVEL

JOE SCHREIBER

BALLANTINE BOOKS • NEW YORK

Chasing the Dead is a work of fiction. Names, characters, places, and incidents are the products of the author's imagination or are used fictitiously. Any resemblance to actual events, locales, or persons, living or dead, is entirely coincidental.

2007 Ballantine Books Mass Market Edition

Copyright © 2006 by Joe Schreiber
Excerpt from *Eat the Dark* copyright © 2007 by Joe Schreiber

Published in the United States by Ballantine Books, an imprint of The Random House Publishing Group, a division of Random House, Inc., New York.

BALLANTINE and colophon are registered trademarks of Random House, Inc.

Originally published in hardcover in the United States by Ballantine Books, an imprint of The Random House Publishing Group, a division of Random House, Inc., in 2006.

ISBN 978-0-345-48748-3

Cover design and illustration: David Stevenson, based on a photograph © Peter Cade/Getty Images

Printed in the United States of America

www.ballantinebooks.com

OPM 9 8 7 6 5 4 3 2 1

To Christina, who had to know how it ended

ACKNOWLEDGMENTS

This book has two champions: Phyllis Westberg and Keith Clayton. Without them the dead within these pages never would have seen the light of day.

For their input and support over the years I am grateful to my friends on both coasts: Michael and Judy Ludy, Jen O'Donohue, Ambrose Wm. Seward, Dan Sklar, Martin Sweeney, and Matt Ware.

Throughout all of this, my amazing children, Jack and Veda, have never stopped asking for scary stories. Kids: Thanks for listening.

Finally, this story and its author owe an incalculable debt of thanks to Betsy Dangel and her son Alexander, in loving memory of Jerry.

The man on the ground has finally stopped moving. The boy looks down at him and uncurls his fingers, allowing the knife to slip from his hand. The blade strikes the packed dirt with a dull thud. The girl next to him hears the noise and flinches. Above them the shadows of late August hang low in the damp air.

The girl looks down at the man. "Is he dead?"

The boy is breathing hard, staring at the knife on the ground. He still feels as if he's ramming it home, over and over, through the shredded denim of the man's bib overalls and deep into the hollow of the man's chest. He can't imagine now where he found the strength to do that. The muscles in his arms are as limp as wet towels, barely capable of supporting the weight of his own hands.

"Is he—"

"Yeah," the boy says. "He's dead."

The girl's eyes widen a fraction, showing extra white along the rims. She has dark blond hair and a pretty face that finds its center in her eyes, green and bright. But the remains of baby fat in her cheeks and the size of her lips have other kids making fun of her at school, calling her Duck-girl or Fat Ass or worse. "What do we do? Should we call the cops?"

The boy doesn't move, staring down at the body below him. He's eleven years old, an age when such focused immobility still seems out of place, even in a kid with such a slight build and intense eyes. "No way," he says quietly. "No cops."

"We can explain it to them. They'll see it and they'll understand."

He shakes his head. "We can't."

"Why not?"

"Look at it." He points with his chin. "I mean, jeez, look what I just did. What if we were wrong? What if—what if it wasn't him?"

"It is him," the girl says. "It's him. It's gotta be. You know it is."

"Yeah, but the *cops* . . . ?" His voice dribbles away and he just looks at her helplessly, wanting to make her agree with him but unable to find the words. "This isn't what I thought was gonna happen," he says finally. "I mean, you saw it, didn't you? Didn't you see what just *happened*?"

The girl stares back at him, tilting her head down a little to meet his eyes, her gaze steadier. They are the same age, in the same grade, but she is almost two inches taller than he is this summer. It will be another year before he catches up with her. After that he'll sprout up, putting on weight and muscle, and she'll be looking up at him for the rest of their lives.

"All right," she says. "Okay, no cops. But what are we going to do?"

The boy glances up at the plastic garbage bags that line the steel mesh trash receptacles along the empty stretch of dirt. He turns slowly, as if in a dream, to the long country road beyond it. Town is a good four miles away, to the north. A hundred yards down the road and to the west, the outline of the old covered bridge rises into the muggy air. The river that runs beneath it, he knows, is as slow and dozy as the August afternoon itself.

"I have an idea," he says.

S tuck in week-before-Christmas traffic north of Boston, Sue Young is scanning the radio dial, searching for a weather report, when a song comes on from the summer of 1983, Duran Duran doing "Rio," and oh boy, does it take her back. Without wanting to, she thinks of Phillip, something he'd said to her once: *The past is never done with us in any substantial way. The most cursory examination reveals its bloody fingerprints on every surface of our lives.*

It's Phillip in a nutshell, an appetizer of eloquent wisdom with a nice fluffy side salad of pomposity. In the beginning, back when they were kids, she'd only heard the wisdom. Later, after they got married, only the pomposity. Now that he's gone Sue hears a dollop of both but mainly she just hears him, his voice in her head, and despite everything he's done to her, she even misses it from time to time.

The song on the radio keeps playing. Sue realizes she's stiffened instinctively against the nice leather upholstery that Phillip paid extra to have installed in the Expedition, not enjoying the crawling prickle of nostalgia, at the same time peripherally aware that traffic is beginning to slide forward in front of her. She starts punching presets on the radio dial as she gooses the gas pedal, picking up speed in little doses, and realizes that the Saturn in front of her has stopped suddenly. She slams on the brakes, the Expedition jerking to a halt just six inches from the Saturn's back bumper, close enough to see the driver's aggrieved expression in the sideview mirror. Sue exhales, thinking that she just used up all her luck for the rest of the night.

It is six twenty and almost totally dark.

Boston is still right there in her rearview, its stumpy conglomeration of mid-rises too close to even be called a skyline. Around her three lanes of commuter traffic slink forward promisingly and then congeal again. To her right, the fax machine that Phillip installed in the Expedition gives two cheerful chirps and starts spitting out a flurry of pages. Sue flips on the dome light and glances at the cover sheet. It's a draft of the loan agreement for her to look over for tomorrow morning's meeting with BayState, the final phase of the Flaherty deal.

Sean Flaherty is an orthodontist, a friend of Phillip's from back in Phillip's bachelor days, when Sean and Phillip chased cocktail waitresses from here to Cape Cod and jetted off to Club Med together to drive Jet Skis and spend their money. Sue actually doesn't mind Sean all that much—he can be a bit overbearing at times, but ever since Phillip left her, Sean's become more subdued, almost shy, around her, as if embarrassed by his old friend's behavior.

Sean has always wanted to open a little bar downtown, in a narrow old space on 151 Exeter Street that he's been lusting after for at least a decade. For years Phillip promised Sean he'd get him 151 Exeter, which has been tied up in probate for ages since the previous owner died intestate and the offspring squabbled over the inheritance. But in the end, the promise to get Sean his bar turned out to be just another broken vow Phillip left in his wake when he abandoned Sue eighteen months ago.

In the end it was Sue herself who closed the deal for Sean, just today. Upon hearing the news Sean dropped by the office, ecstatic, with two freshly steamed lobsters and a gift-wrapped case of liquor that he insisted Sue take home with her. Sue was happy to accept the lobsters, but she hasn't had anything stronger than club soda in five years. She hadn't even bothered unwrapping it to see what it was. And right now, as the traffic shifts forward and the bottles in the back of the Expedition clink softly together, she wonders what on earth she's going to do with an entire case of hard liquor. It's too late to give it out for Christmas. Does Goodwill accept alcohol?

She reaches over and pulls out her cell phone from her coat pocket. It would be easier to pick up the car phone mounted in the Expedition, just twelve inches away from the steering wheel. But she's so in the habit of using her cell—sometimes it feels grafted between her shoulder and her jaw—that she'll often catch herself using it even when she's home sitting right in front of the land line.

Sue hits the programmed number for the house and waits, but there's no answer. No messages from Marilyn on her voicemail or the machine. No text messages except Brad at work reminding her about the bank meeting with Sean tomorrow morning to close on his bar. She dials the number in the Jeep and after three rings Marilyn picks up with a disorganized-sounding "hello."

"Hey," Sue says, "it's me."

"Oh, hey, hi."

Sue checks the clock again even though she just did it twenty seconds earlier. It's a habit with her. Time is a rival. "You headed out for dinner?"

"Actually just getting back," Marilyn says, and in the background Sue can hear Veda doing a running commentary in the blithe, hyperinflective nonsense of toddler argot. "Her Creative Movements class ran a little late and we ended up grabbing an early dinner at the Rainforest Cafe. Should be home in twenty minutes or so."

"So you already ate?"

"Yeah."

Sue looks at the Legal Seafood box on the floor next to her, the one that Sean had produced with such pleasure that she couldn't help getting caught up in his excitement. "Too bad for you. Somebody gave me a couple of lobsters." It's the sort of remark that invites questions—somebody gave you *lobsters?*—but she only hears Marilyn grunt on the other end, uncharacteristically quiet, distracted. A red light goes on in Sue's mind. "Is everything all right?"

"Yeah," Marilyn says, "this loser in a van is just riding my tail. Sorry."

"I'll let you go."

"We'll see you back at the house," Marilyn says, and clicks off. Sue drops the phone on top of her coat, folded on the passenger seat, and concentrates on her driving. It isn't snowing, not yet, but it still takes her the better part of an hour to get back to Concord and by the time she pulls up to the house she's hungry and frustrated enough that she forgets the lobsters and the liquor in the car.

Inside, it takes her a moment before she realizes that Marilyn and Veda aren't home yet. She kicks off her shoes and calls the Jeep's phone again but this time nobody answers.

Odd, she thinks, heading into the kitchen. Not alarming, necessarily, but definitely out of character for Marilyn, who wouldn't normally deviate from the plan without letting Sue know. Marilyn's been Sue's nanny for over a year now and they work well together because they think alike. Veda loves Marilyn, and that's terrific, that's a real plus. But at the end of the day what matters is that Marilyn and Sue share the same peculiarities, the same worries, the same little neuroses about raising a child in a world where handguns cost less than a pair of sneakers and nobody washes their hands. When the agency first sent her over for an interview, Sue took Marilyn out to lunch and watched her use her hip to bump open the ladies' room door so that she could keep her hands clean. Sue made her an offer before their salads arrived.

The phone rings as she's pouring herself a cranberry juice and tonic with a wedge of lime.

"Hello?"

A man's voice, one she doesn't know. "Susan Young?"

"Speaking," she says, already thinking: *telemarketer.* She hasn't been Susan to anybody but distant relatives since eighth grade. There's still half a chicken Caesar in the fridge from last night at the Capital Grille and she opens the Styrofoam box with the phone tucked under her jaw, picking off slightly soggy croutons and cherry tomatoes.

"Is this Susan?" the man asks again with irritating slowness.

"Yes, this is she. Who's calling?"

"You have a very lovely little girl, Susan."

And Sue freezes, feeling the tiles of the kitchen floor vanish beneath her feet. "Who is this?"

"She's beautiful. Gorgeous green eyes, precious blond hair, those little dimples on the backs of her hands when she uncurls her fingers. And that smile, Susan. She certainly favors you." The voice pauses. "Susan? Are you there?"

S ue doesn't say anything. Can't, really. Standing in the middle of her kitchen, gazing out the window where her three acres of dark woods slope away underneath the moonlight, she's hearing things in the man's voice, a barely suppressed note of hilarity underneath what she first thought was a toneless growl. She can hear him breathe between phrases, as if it's difficult for him to get whole sentences out without inhaling. There are no other sounds in the background.

Somehow she has the presence of mind to think that when things like this happen in the movies or on TV the person's first response is to accuse the caller of playing some kind of joke, or to get angry and accuse them of lying. But somehow she knows that this is not a joke and the man on the phone isn't lying to her. And anger is a long, long way from what she's feeling right now.

"I haven't lost you, have I, Susan?"

No, she tries to say but no noise comes out. There

is still the sense of not touching anything, not even the clothes she's wearing. In fact she is floating, suspended in a gel of utter disbelief, not even horrified yet, although the horror is certainly out there and she can feel it corroding its way inward. "No," she says again, louder. "Who is this?"

"We'll get there," the man says. "We've got all night. And after all this is December twenty-first. The longest night of the year."

She has absolutely no idea how to respond to that observation. "Is she there?" she asks. "Is my daughter there with you?"

"Of course she is, Susan. You don't think I'd leave a little one-year-old unattended, do you?"

"Where's Marilyn?"

The man hesitates like he has to think about it. "Oh," he says, "she's here, too. We're all here, Susan."

"Let me talk to my daughter. Please."

"I'll put her on soon, I promise. Before that we need to establish a few ground rules. You've got a long way to go in the next twelve hours. It will make everything much easier and that way there won't be any misunderstandings between us later on." The man is speaking a bit quicker now, out of excitement, she senses. "First, it's important that you don't call the police. Not that I don't trust you, Susan, but you should know that I have tapped your phone and I'm scanning your cell, so if you make any calls to anyone, I'll know. Now I'm going to hang up and wait, and if you've followed rule number one, then in ten minutes

I'll call back and we'll go from there. Are you with me so far?"

"Wait—"

"I'll take that as a yes," he says, and hangs up on her, gone, just like that. She stands there with the phone buzzing in her hand and then it leaps upon her, the fullness of it, with all its weight. She has never been one to absorb things gradually. When the unexpected happens she would always rather grapple with it immediately and to hell with denial, anger, and all those other stages of acceptance.

The room begins to tilt and she feels her knees buckle as she sinks to the floor still clutching the phone, realizing she's not breathing yet unable to will herself to inhale. From somewhere deep in her chest she hears the low, slow whine of her lungs pleading for air. Instead she begins slowly and deliberately to bring order to the available facts. She forces herself to think rationally. She hears Marilyn's voice on the phone from an hour earlier:

This loser in a van is just riding my tail.

The realization kicks the door wide open to a blizzard of images. The man who was following her forcing the Jeep off the road, dragging Marilyn from behind the wheel, putting a gun to her head, and forcing her out of the car. Climbing into the Jeep with Veda still strapped into her car seat, Veda facing backward, her round, mostly bald head cocked in confusion and alarm at her nanny's screams and cries for help, the faceless one putting the vehicle in gear and driving off into the night. The man and Sue's daughter somewhere out on the freeway now, somewhere in the black expanse of a New England winter—

The phone rings again and Sue almost screams.

S he drops it, picks it up again, and hits the talk button: "Yes."

"Hey, Susie-Q. You sound stressed, babe, you okay?" It's a different man's voice, smoother, familiar, and through her panic Sue realizes that it's Brad from the office. "Listen, just a couple quick questions about the bank meeting tomorrow morning—"

"I can't talk right now."

"What's wrong?" He's dropped the hipster affectation for a more genuine concern, but Sue's already hanging up on him, still crouched down so that her kitchen and dining room sprawl high above her. She assumes the world looks like this to Veda all the time. The ceiling just goes up and up. She has another vivid flash of her daughter in her car seat, scared and crying inconsolably, and feels her jaw yawn wide to let out an aching scream that comes out more like a sob.

Through all the crazy shifts she's worked at Commonwealth Emergency Response and the death and bloodshed she's witnessed in those early days, only once has Sue experienced anything of this intensity, a hot summer afternoon that she scarcely remembers except on the most subconscious level. Yet in some terribly practical way that experience has inoculated her against certain dangerous extremes—the very real possibility of losing herself to hysteria, for example. Even now she has found that she does not get hysterical, and in a moment her breathing has restored itself to a shallow but steady rhythm.

The phone rings again. She goes flopping across the floor as if struck by a cattle prod but this time she does not scream.

"Hello."

"Who was that, Susan?" the voice asks.

"Brad. He works at my office. I didn't tell him anything."

"I know," the voice says. "I told you I would be listening. You were a very good girl. It was an unexpected test, but you passed with flying colors. I believe you're ready to move to the next level. What do you think?"

"Please, just let me talk to her." It is so deadly quiet on his end, with only his voice relayed to her through the shallow acoustics of a wireless line, the closest thing she can imagine to hearing voices in your own head. "Just for a second. May I, please?"

"Absolutely," he says. "Didn't I promise I'd let you do that? I always keep my promises, Susan." And there's a rustle of fabric or skin against the mouthpiece, then a silence, followed by soft, intent breathing that she recognizes instantly as her daughter's.

And just like that Sue Young's hard-won composure disappears.

She just melts.

"Veda, honey?" she says. "It's Mommy, baby. Sweetie, can you hear me? *Veda . . . ?*" She feels the tears swell up behind her eyes, pressure mounting in her chest like a balloon expanding between her lungs and ribs, filling her with all the horror and fear in the world until it's leaking out her eyes and nose and mouth. "Veda, it's going to be all right, honey, Mommy promises, everything's going to be okay, okay?"

Veda makes one of her sounds, a repeating two-syllable noise coiled in puzzlement—dukka-*dukka?*—and that does it. The fear and grief just take over. Sue breaks down. Tears stream down and the screams start backing up in her throat and somehow she manages to hold her breath for one more second because she wants to hear if Veda says anything else. But there is nothing else coming, just another rustling sound and the voice coming back on, sounding deeply pleased with itself.

"She's very good with strangers," he observes, almost mildly.

Sue forces herself to stop crying, bites her lip, balls her left hand into a fist, and mashes it to her mouth. "Anything," she says finally. She can taste blood mixed with tears and her lip aches faintly from biting it. Her chest, her face, her throat all ache. "Anything you want. Just please, don't hurt her."

"I told you, we'll get to that. You passed the first

test, Susan, but I just need to be absolutely sure that I can trust you not to call the police."

"I won't. I swear."

No answer.

"You want money," she says. "I can give you however much you want. Just name your price."

"You're not listening to me." Abruptly the voice has taken a nasty turn. "I'm assuming that you're smart, Susan, but right now you're losing IQ points by the second. Now, if you want to see your daughter alive, then shut up and listen." He doesn't wait for any acknowledgment beyond her silence. "All right. Are you ready to listen and do what I tell you?"

"Yes."

"Good. You're going to go outside and get in your car. I'm giving you ten seconds to get out there. Are you ready?"

"Yes."

"Go."

He hangs up and she drops the cordless, pivots, and bolts out of the kitchen and down the hall in her stocking feet, jumping out the front door and down the driveway. The darkness and cold against her skin don't even register. The door latch on the Expedition catches the first time and she jerks it again, jumps behind the wheel, and grabs the car phone, which is already ringing. Like the radio it is designed to carry a residual charge allowing for its use even when the motor isn't running.

"I'm here," she says.

"Start the engine."

Sue gropes instinctively for the ignition and finds nothing but air. The keys aren't there. Of course they aren't. She brought them into the house with her and dropped them on the counter right before taking off her shoes. She feels a cramp of dread and improbable embarrassment. "I didn't bring my keys."

"Susan, shame on you. You used to drive an ambulance for a living, how could you forget your *keys*?"

"How do you know that?"

He ignores her. "I guess you don't have to be rich for very long before you start forgetting all the practicalities of daily living, isn't that right?"

She doesn't answer. What's she supposed to say?

"That's all right, Susan. I'll give you another chance. I'm a big believer in second chances. What about you? Do *you* believe in second chances?"

"Yes."

"Good. Right now I just need you to sit here like a good girl. Can you do that for me?"

"Yes," she says, and for the first time, sitting out in the darkness of the Expedition, which is still warm and smells like the steamed lobsters she left out here by accident, she thinks that the voice on the phone is familiar somehow, from a long time ago. She does not know where or when—her mind will not grant her access to that information—but the familiarity nags just the same, and she thinks again about the idea of voices in her head.

"I'm holding a knife in my right hand," the voice says casually. "It's a hunting knife, one of my favorites. I've had it for many years, but it's still fairly new and in excellent shape. It's stainless steel with a nine-inch blade. It's terribly sharp."

Sue hears herself trying not to make a sound. She makes one anyway, an awful-sounding groan. If he hears this on his end, he doesn't comment.

"Now I'm going to make another promise. In exactly twelve hours, I'm going to plant this knife in little Veda's throat. The police will never find her body and you will never see her again, but for the rest of your life you will know exactly how she died, and her blood will be on your hands. And how will you know that?"

Sue waits, not getting it. Then she understands. "Because," she says, "because you always keep your promises?"

"That's right, Susan! You remembered that! That's very good!" She can almost hear the grin in his voice. "There's hope for you yet, I think. Now, as I said, the only way that this isn't going to happen is if you do exactly what I tell you. The choice is yours, but I'm going to suggest that you don't waste any more time bargaining with me or offering me money. And I especially don't want to hear any more pointless questions. I'll give you all the information you need. That means all you have to do is listen to what I tell you and do what I want. Do you understand?"

"Yes," she says. "Yes, yes."

"Good. You're going to go back into the house and get your jacket and boots. Get a pair of gloves, a flashlight, and a shovel—the one from the garden shed, not the snow shovel. Are you getting all this, Susan?"

"How do you know about . . . ?" She stops, catching herself. Then it hits her. Has he actually been inside her house?

"Get the nylon rope from the hook in the garage, and the canvas folded up in the shed. Take all of it and put it in the back of the Expedition. I'm going to call again in three minutes. If you're not back behind the wheel in time with everything you need, you'll miss my call and you'll never hear from me or little Veda again. You don't want that to happen, do you?"

"That's not enough time."

"What did I say about bargaining? You're not listening to me, Susan. These terms aren't negotiable. The only decision you have to make is whether you want to see Veda again."

"All right," she says softly.

"Good. And Susan?"

"Yes?"

"This time, don't forget the car keys."

And he's gone.

7:40 P.M.

She springs out of the Expedition and hits the ground running. In her mind she is already poring over the list of items he named, organizing them according to where they are in the house. She is good at this, in a sense it is what she has always done best—track, prioritize, multitask, always with one eye on the clock.

In the first sixty seconds she has her coat, gloves, boots, keys, and the flashlight all tucked into her pockets. She swings through the garage for the rope and sprints across the yard through the darkness to the garden shed, the one that Phillip built for them their first summer here in Concord, two years ago. It turned out to be their only summer together, but the tools he bought for her are all still here, many of them unused, each hanging neatly on its nail.

She takes down the shovel, turns, and aims the flashlight down in the corner but the sheet of canvas she keeps there to cover the flower beds is gone. There is a clean rectangle of cement where it normally lies, where she knows—flat-out *knows*—that it should be. But it is not there. And it is not there, of course, because the man on the phone took it when he came out here and inventoried her belongings, some hours or days or even weeks ago. Intuitively Sue senses this is because he wants her to know that he's been here, that he does not want to leave any doubt about it.

Time, she thinks, and runs back as fast as she can, bypassing the house entirely this time, which is a mistake. It is quite dark now, and the only light source in the backyard is the faint yellowish illumination bleeding from the kitchen window, just above the sink. When she rounds the side of the house she trips on something and goes flying, landing hard on the palms of her hands, hearing her own breath go out of her with a muffled *guff*. She hears her keys jingling somewhere beside her. She gropes the cold blades of grass in front of her in search of the flashlight, but that's gone too and for a moment she's skating wildly toward the edge of panic. She can hear the phone chirping inside the Expedition down in the driveway. It sounds hugely, massively, dreamily far away.

It hasn't been three minutes yet. It hasn't even been close.

Standing up, Sue spins around and catches the gleam of the flashlight in the grass and switches it on, splashing it over the yard in search of the keys. The phone is still ringing in the Expedition: the third ring dwindling away, a silence, and the fourth ring starting. She can see the flashlight beam trembling as her whole body shakes harder in the cadence of some accelerated pounding within. Her heart is a lunatic banging on a metal can. It is like swimming to the surface with her lungs bursting for air, kicking furiously, but the surface just keeps pulling farther away from her no matter how hard she struggles for it. Finally with an audible curse Sue gives up looking for the lost keys, wrenches herself forward, running for the Expedition, and diving inside to snatch the phone from the passenger seat where she'd abandoned it. She doesn't even have enough air in her lungs to speak, just gasps, trying not to pass out.

"You made it," he says, as if expecting nothing less.

"I don't," she says, and swallows dryly, "have my keys. I'm sorry. I tripped. I don't know where they went, I couldn't . . ."

Her voice trails off and the silence that follows it is endless, fathomless. When the voice speaks again there is a hollow darkness within it that chills her to her very soul.

"That's too bad, Susan. I guess we can't play after all."

"Wait."

"I gave you clear instructions. All you've done is disappoint me."

"Please—"

"Listen closely now, because you're about to hear me slit your baby's throat."

"*No!*"

"Too late, Susan."

"Stop it!" She jerks straight upright in the front seat, both hands clutching helplessly at the phone as if she could somehow reach through and rescue Veda, and her coat flap catches on her left sleeve. As the edge of the coat flips up, its outer pocket tips sideways and her keys spill out along with her gloves, bouncing off her knee and falling to the floor.

You put them in your pocket. That's where they were the whole time, stuffed between your gloves where you couldn't hear them jingling.

"Wait!" she shouts, ramming her hand down below her feet, fingers probing, encountering the little metal ridges hooked to the reassuring weight of the clicker, right there in her palm. "I have them! They were in my pocket! I have them!"

She slips the key into the ignition, the dashboard brightening obediently in front of her.

"Hello?" she says. "Are you there? Can you hear me?"

She listens. For an eternity, nothing. Then:

"Do you have everything else?" he asks.

She thinks of the canvas tarp, and the shovel for that matter, which ended up somewhere in the side yard when she fell on her face. But there is no margin for error, she judges, not now, perhaps not ever again. "Yes," she lies smoothly.

"Are you sure?"

"Yes."

There is a pause long enough that she has to wrestle to control her trembling for fear that he can hear it in her respiration. Despite the cold she can feel a droplet of sweat leaking from her right armpit down her ribs. "All right, then." He sounds convinced, or wants her to think that he is. Either way it is no longer of any consequence. "Start the car and head east toward Route 2. Get off on 23 and look for the sign for Everett Road. When you get there you're going to head north. I'll call you again when you get there. And remember, Susan."

"What?"

"You have a job to do. I'll be watching you. If you make any unauthorized stops to ask for help or use a pay phone, I will cut your little girl up and send you the pieces. Do you believe me?"

"Yes."

"Are you sure?"

"Yes."

"Good. We'll be in touch."

"When will you—"

Click. He's gone.

For the first few minutes, she just drives. She does not permit herself to think. Not about Marilyn, not about the voice, and most of all, not about Veda. Not yet.

Traffic is still heavy on Route 2 but at least it's moving. People are getting back to their homes, settling in for the evening, switching on the TV, perhaps pouring themselves a glass of wine. For those unfortunate enough to be on the road, the first few white flakes are starting to sift down, bouncing off her windshield as she heads north. Eventually she gets off on Everett Road, two lanes of nothing much at all.

Her mind drifts slightly. It is not advisable, this drifting, but there it is.

She cannot help but think what it would be like if Phillip were here.

The temptation to try to call him, to grab the phone and punch in the West Coast number he left on her machine a year or so ago, six months after stepping permanently out of her life, is far stronger than any urge to call the police. Sue does not have much faith in the police. She doesn't exactly have a whole lot of faith in Phillip, either—what can you say about a man who abandons his wife and one-month-old daughter, even if he leaves them with a yacht, an *Architectural Digest* home, and full ownership of the third largest real estate office in Boston?

Abandoned is abandoned, as her friend Natalie is fond of saying, and scum is scum. Of course Natalie always sounds a little envious when she says this, like she wouldn't mind finding out firsthand what it's like being abandoned with a big house and millions of dollars to spend, but Sue is not even remotely deluded about the emotional fallout of Phillip's disappearance. She knows that Veda will grow up without a father, nothing more than a tall, narrow-shouldered shadow with graying hair leaning over her bassinet on the videotape that Sue has no intention of ever allowing her daughter to watch.

But the fact is that Phillip Chamberlain has been a part of her life for almost as far back as Sue can remember. In elementary school back in their hometown of Gray Haven, Massachusetts, they were the two classic pillars upon which the caste system rested: Nerd Boy and Fat Girl. They've been through the shit together. By tenth grade Sue thinned out and sprouted breasts, and the big lips that had once been the object of such unimaginative scorn were regarded with admiration, jealousy, and flat-out lust. Meanwhile it was obvious to everyone that the reason Phillip didn't give a rat's ass what anybody thought was because he was smart enough to do whatever he wanted. And the first thing he wanted was to get out of Gray Haven.

But even after he started getting scholarship offers to Harvard, Princeton, and Stanford, and she was turning down dates from quarterbacks, the glue between them—the intractable outsiders' bond—had only grown stronger. They tried being boyfriend and girlfriend for a while, even made out a few times in the backseat of Phillip's Toyota—it seemed like Extreme's "More Than Words" was always playing on the stereo—but it was always easier being friends.

With that in mind, somebody once remarked (was it Phillip himself?) that their eventual marriage was built more on inevitability than any sort of romance or even affection. Certainly there *was* plenty of affection too, maybe even a little steamy romance in their backseat mash sessions. But more than anything there was just the sense of having been there for each other during a particularly awful period of their lives, a moment so horrible that you needed to share it with somebody or else it would destroy you.

After high school there was a ten-year-plus lull when they rarely saw each other. Phillip graduated from Harvard and began buying apartment buildings around town, little ones and then big ones. Sue dropped out of college and started driving an ambulance for a living, a job she found just crazy enough to temporarily satisfy the chaos-addict that she'd discovered lurking inside herself. Throughout the nineties they kept in touch via phone calls, Christmas cards, and e-mails, along with that occasional moment of ESP when she was sure that he was thinking about her at the same moment she was thinking about him. She worked maniacal hours, dated the usual string of police-scanner geeks and buzz-cut paramedics, went to bars, took drugs, and woke up in too many different places without knowing exactly where her clothes were.

That period of her life had bottomed out on one Fourth of July weekend on the night she tried to drive home from Singing Beach, blind drunk, to the vacation condo she was renting in Beverly Farms. Despite the fact that the road refused to hold still, ambulance-driver bravado carried the day and she was sure she could make it, right up to the moment her old Jeep Wrangler left the road and rolled over three times before hitting a tree. Sue spent six hours in the OR but made it out alive, scared, scarred, and sober. It was all very *Behind the Music,* but no less effective for all of that, a reminder that when life wants to get our attention it doesn't bother with half-measures. Eight months later she ran into Phillip at a Super Bowl party at a mutual friend's house. They ended up back at his brownstone on Beacon Hill, where he said nothing about the scars running up her abdomen and cleaving her right nipple in half, but only kissed her and held her in his arms. And Sue would be lying if she didn't admit, at least to herself, that the first emotion that she felt was a sense of relief, of finally being home.

Six months later she was pregnant with Veda. The sensible thing, Phillip said, was to get married so Sue could quit her job and they could get busy taking vacations, spending the money he was making, and spoiling their kid. Sue surprised herself by saying okay. That was a little over two years ago, when they were both in their early thirties. He was already running a multimillion-dollar real estate business out of his office in Cambridge, holding business meetings by cell phone from his Boston Whaler, or telecommuting from his house on Nantucket—all of which, upon edict from Phillip's lawyers, now belongs to Sue. Phillip has seen to that, shifting ownership of everything to Sue in the seemingly endless jet stream of phone calls, e-mails, legal documents, and bank transfers sweeping out of Malibu over the first twelve months immediately following his departure. Throughout this last summer communications between them dwindled to a trickle, as the last loose ends were tied up, everything going into Sue's name. She hasn't heard from him at all since September, not even a Christmas card. And though he is scum for leaving, she can't help but think that having him here might somehow reassure her that she isn't losing her mind.

The notion evaporates, and she is just driving again. After a moment she tastes salt.

She realizes that she is thinking about Veda, and weeping.

And just like that, the phone is in her hand.

It occurs to her that the man's threat of listening in on her calls could be a bluff, but probably not. After all, she owns a baby monitor, and she's been on her cell phone and heard snatches of her own conversation crackling through Veda's bedroom enough times that she doesn't even use the cell inside the house when her daughter is upstairs napping. And the paramedics and ham radio operators that she's dated used to entertain themselves for hours listening in on other people's calls, miles away. It not only *could* happen; it happened all the time.

Then you have to assume that he is listening. All the time.

But in the silent emptiness of the wooded road around her, the thought of calling Phillip refuses to go away. What if she were to call him and have *him* call the police, using some kind of code that Veda's abductor might not recognize, and then hang up? She already knows what she could say, the phrase that would send up a red flag for him, without alerting the man on the phone what she was talking about.

She picks up the phone.

Don't be stupid. Is it really worth risking Veda's life for this?

What if she doesn't say a word? She could just dial his number. He'd see it on his caller ID, and—

Then she sees them, a half mile back.

Headlights.

I'm watching you.

They're coming up fast, too fast, swooping to narrow the distance between them in what seems like a split second, already close enough to drag her shadow upward across the dashboard.

Sue shoves the phone down between the seats as the headlights swallow her. She can hear the engine, an irregular *BLAT BLAT BLAT* that sounds more like a single-engine plane than a car. Now it is alongside her, and she sees it's a truck, actually, but the driver's face is obscured as it plows past her and swings up in front, cutting her off.

Sue hits the brakes, dropping back, tasting a sudden reflux of fear. Brake lights flare in front of her, forcing her to slow even more. Her tires squeal; the seat belt catches her hard and makes her sternum ache. The box containing the steamed lobsters tips up on its side and she hears them flop over sideways with a thump. Up ahead of her, twenty feet away, the truck has come to a complete stop, its engine throbbing. It is one of those old no-color farm pickups with rounded corners, a great grinning grille, and something boisterously wrong with its muffler.

She can feel the driver's eyes gleaming in his side-view mirror, reflected back at her in the volcanic-black darkness. Examining her face.

Then she can't move.

She *recognizes* this truck. She's seen it before. Now that it's right in front of her, she's almost positive that it's the same one that—

The phone rings.

8:18 P.M.

"Hello?"

"Susan."

"I'm . . . please, I'm sorry. I slipped. It was a mistake."

"Susan."

"Don't hurt her. Do whatever you want to me. I'm sorry. I swear it won't happen again. Just please—"

"*Susan.*"

Her teeth snap shut. She closes her eyes. She cannot bear the moist optic glimmer that she senses coming from the pickup's eccentrically tooled sideview mirrors, those dark eyes shining like tumors from their rusty chrome sockets.

The driver's side door opens and a man steps out. His face is lost in the darkness, but she can tell from the angle of his head and shoulders that he's looking straight at her. Snowflakes spill through the headlights aiming off into the woods.

Holding the phone very close to her ear, Sue says, "Please. Please don't hurt her."

For a moment the man doesn't move. He seems to

be watching her even more closely, as if trying to make a decision about something. Then he gets back up behind the wheel and slams the door.

"Thank you," she says. "Thank you so m—"

The truck spins its tires and lurches back into motion, its motor pounding off down the highway in a steadily diminishing array of asymmetric taillights. It leaves her there clutching the phone, not sure whether the voice is still with her or not. In the silence she realizes she can hear him breathing.

"You've made it this far," the voice says. "But so far it's been relatively easy. What you're going to do next isn't going to be nearly so easy. But I know you can do it, Susan." And does he actually chuckle? "I have faith in you."

She waits. He does not make her wait long.

"You're familiar with Route 114, aren't you?"

"Yes."

"It runs east and west, right along the state line. If you follow it far enough to the east it takes you out to the coast. But you're going to start out by taking it west. Back to a little town called Gray Haven. You do know Gray Haven, don't you, Susan?"

"Of course." Her voice feels detached from her, like something recorded a long time ago and played back. It doesn't sound like her at all. "I grew up there."

"That's right, Susan. You grew up there. In fact, you left something behind and tonight, you're going to get it back."

"I don't know what you're talking about."

"I don't know what you're talking about," he mim-

ics cruelly, and it seems like he should be laughing, but he's not. There is no hint of humor, not even sarcasm, in his voice. It's like before, when it turned nasty, but this is much, much worse. "You listen to me, you worthless little cunt, because I'm only going to say this once. The only thing you're doing when you play dumb is putting this knife closer to little Veda's throat. Now, do you know what I'm talking about?"

There's another pause, Sue leaning forward into the phone, and in the background, horribly, she can hear Veda again, starting to cry in a shrill wail. It is not a cry of fear now, but unquestionably a cry of pain.

"Wait, please, stop!" Sue shouts, tears in her eyes again, voice going to pieces. "I'll do whatever you want! Just please don't hurt her anymore!"

He doesn't answer her and she's left with the sound of Veda crying louder. Sue feels the abrupt soreness in her breasts and the left cup of her bra is wet with milk from her undamaged left nipple, the left breast being the only one able to produce milk for Veda after the accident. She hasn't nursed her daughter in almost six months but her body doesn't seem to care about this. Sue is still crying too, unable to control herself, and the next voice she hears isn't the man on the phone at all. It's Phillip's voice, in her head, calm and clear and in its way almost as real as the one coming through the cell phone.

Stop it, Sue. Just stop it, right now.

She catches her breath. In spite of everything, she's startled into silence at how vividly she can hear him.

This is bad. It's the worst. But nothing's ever been solved with tears. So just . . . stop . . . crying.

"All right," she whispers. Not whimpers, just whispers. And in a moment she has nearly regained the fullness of her voice. Through the receiver she can hear her daughter still crying, but she's calmed down a bit too, thank God, and it sounds as if whatever the man on the other end was doing to her has stopped, at least for now. Maybe he was just pinching her, she thinks. Maybe not even that. If Marilyn really is there, maybe she was somehow able to protect Veda. Or comfort her. Marilyn would do anything for Veda, Sue knows, putting her own life on the line for Veda if that is what it takes.

At least this is what she chooses to believe, for this very moment at hand, and if it gets her through to the next moment, then she may continue to believe it.

"A long time ago," the voice on the phone says, "you and your friend did something that neither one of you will ever forget. You do know who I'm talking about, Susan. You know very well."

Sue Young sits perfectly still like a figure in a snow globe, amid the increasing chaos of tumbling white, staring out the windshield at the bare trees along the road, a dense thicket of questions tightening around her like some kind of barbwire shroud.

"Yes."

How does the voice on the other end know about this? It is one thing to know about her life now, where she works, where she lives, and what kind of car she drives. Even to have gone into her house and looked through her things—an intruder with enough intelligence and motive could have done that.

But nobody knows about what they did that summer, the thing that bonded them together permanently. In a peculiar way, she herself doesn't know about it. It has not been on her mind, at least the daytime part of her mind, since she graduated high school. In fact, it is as if some arcane form of psychological self-defense had wiped him completely from her consciousness even before she left Gray Haven.

Phillip, she knows, has not been so lucky.

For whatever reason—perhaps just because he is a man and not so consciously accustomed to the sprockets and flywheels of psychological micromanagement—he has not been able to expel the nightmares so handily. Only after they were married did she realize that he still had nightmares about it. They attacked in cycles, serially, industriously corroding whole layers of insulation off his ordered and businesslike thoughts right up until the point that he left her eighteen months ago. Sometimes he'd thrash so violently in bed that she was afraid he might hurt himself, or her. Sometimes he shot straight up in bed with a scream like nothing she'd ever heard from him when he was awake. His eyes were open but he was still dreaming. There was sweat in his hair, pasting it down in thick brown fingers to his forehead. Even when the dreams were at their worst, he refused to tell her about them, but Sue always knew—on the same level that she herself remembers. She knows all this because he is Phillip Chamberlain, the only boy she ever loved, and because they went through it all together, approximately one lifetime ago.

"Tonight you're going back to Gray Haven," the voice says.

"What?"

"You're going back to pay your respects. Do you know the place?"

"Who are you?"

"Answer the question, Susan. Do you know the place?"

"I know the place, but—"

"Good."

Again Sue is silent. In the background she can hear Veda again, not crying but whimpering, tired, hungry, wanting it to be over. *Oh honey, oh sweetie, I sympathize.* And Sue has to hang up on the voice to keep from asking to talk to her baby girl again.

Because she already knows this is how this game will be played.

Whatever privileges she might have had to make special requests are gone.

For the sake of her daughter she is going to do exactly what the voice asked.

She is going back to Gray Haven.

8:42 P.M.

The roads are going to hell. Sue can feel it, that queasy little shimmy in the back tires whenever she adjusts the wheel more than a few degrees in either direction. It's snowing harder now. Still, the Expedition is holding steady at sixty-five, sometimes seventy-five when the road straightens out. She's got another half hour until she gets to Gray Haven, maybe longer if the weather continues to fall apart like it is.

Still, she's had plenty of experience driving under adverse conditions. You can't drive an ambulance for eleven years without experiencing everything that bad weather, bad karma, and plain rotten luck have to offer. Before she left it all behind to become Mrs. Phillip Chamberlain, Sue delivered babies in the middle of electrical storms and drove stroke victims through nor'easters. Once, when her ambulance broke down in the middle of Buttfuck Idaho she and her partner kept an eight-year-old with his throat half torn out by a German shepherd alive and calm for an hour and a half until a helicopter arrived, and the kid eventually recovered enough to send her a crayon-drawn thank-you note. Sue used to keep it stashed above the visor of her ambulance. Back in the day, she was the golden girl—the one everybody said could eat stress and shit sonnets.

The road rises and falls and the opening lines of one of Veda's favorite board books, a story that Sue's read her at least a hundred times, keeps repeating stupidly through her head: *"Up slippery hills cars creep, don't beep. Inside the hills the giants sleep."* It is what you get with kids. The children's authors of America erect a little writer's colony in your forebrain, and no matter how grim or horrific the circumstances you find yourself in, they're always ready with a bit of utterly inappropriate doggerel.

Driving on. She's got the road mainly to herself. She passes several cars, a Dunkin' Donuts truck, even a couple of snowplows, but there's no sign of the farm pickup she saw earlier. The more she thinks about it, the more certain she is that it's the one from two months earlier, the afternoon of the pumpkin patch.

One day back in late October, a week before Halloween, Sue and Marilyn took Veda pumpkin-picking outside Lexington. Veda ran up and down the rows of gnarled green vines and pumpkins, stopping every few feet to attempt to pick one up until she finally found one small enough to lift. The three of them went out to dinner afterward and Veda fell asleep in the car, the crisp air and exercise having done its job. Sue dropped Marilyn back at her condo, then headed back to the house with her sleeping daughter still clutching the miniature pumpkin in her car seat.

They were just a few miles from home, cruising along a backwoods two-lane road, when somebody started flashing their headlights at her from behind. Sue slowed down, thinking the driver wanted to pass, but then he slowed down too, coming up close behind her, and Sue felt all her alarm systems go on at once. The vehicle was an old pickup with a big grille, round fenders, and wide-set headlights, just like the one tonight, and the driver was waving her over to the shoulder.

Maybe, she remembered thinking at the time, the guy was just flagging her down to tell her she had a taillight out or something. But a lonely stretch of road five miles outside of town was the last place she wanted to find out. When the farm pickup slowed down, Sue floored it and lost him, got her little girl home and locked the doors. In the garage she checked the Expedition. The taillights, and everything else, were just fine. And she hadn't seen the farm pickup again until tonight.

But is that really the case?

The headache between her eyes is starting to come back. Because now she's thinking of an evening just a week or so ago when she was downtown doing some Christmas shopping at Prudential Center, pulling out of the parking garage, and a pair of headlights swept out after her. She only got a glimpse of the vehicle before it vanished in traffic, but hadn't it looked like the same farm truck? Hadn't she recognized, just for a split second, that grinning grille and rounded front end?

Even then, the connection between the two events pulsed in and out of her mind and vanished as quickly as it had arrived. Because who would really be following *her*? What were the odds that it was the same truck?

But now she realizes that it was.

How long, exactly, has he been following her?

Again her thoughts go to Marilyn and Sue prays (yes, prays, and any ambulance driver who tells you they've never muttered a prayer is lying, heartless, or both) that somehow the nanny is able to protect Veda or at least reassure her, hold her hand or sing to her. An eighteen-month-old girl can't possibly understand what's happening to her. Sue doesn't know enough about childhood trauma to know if this is a blessing or a curse. She just prays that Marilyn is insulating Veda from the worst of it, that the man who has her has done nothing to either of them physically, prays that despite hearing Veda scream that one time over the phone. But even if he hasn't touched Veda, except for the time he made her cry on the phone, even then, how much therapy will she need as an adult just to get her through the distant memory of this night?

But maybe, just maybe, it's still all right. Maybe Veda's already cried herself out and fallen asleep. It is possible, isn't it? Eight o'clock is her bedtime. Maybe in the morning she'll wake up and Marilyn will be there and Sue will arrive and it will all be like a bad dream.

Or maybe they're already dead.

"Stop that," Sue says aloud to herself. "You stop that shit right now."

But behind that tough snarl—and it is tough, Sue can hear that much just listening to the sound of her own voice—another scared, selfish question hangs, rotating slowly, the one question that she simply cannot help asking on some level. Just two hours earlier she was an affluent thirtysomething-year-old ex-wife and mother, and Veda was just another one-and-a-half-year-old coming home with her nanny to get ready for her nightly bath before bedtime. Why is this happening to them?

Because the past is never done with us. Not in any substantial way.

Screw you, Phillip, Sue thinks. Screw you, you unreliable rat, you child-abandoning shitbag, you worthless waste of skin. You're in Malibu right now, no doubt jogging naked down some beach when you're not mixing up a pitcher of sour apple martinis for your newest surgically enhanced fuck doll while three thousand miles away some faceless maniac does Christ-knows-what to your only daughter. So forgive me if your charming philosophical views on the past don't quite engage me like they used to back in the jolly old days of yore.

Instead Sue thinks of Veda, holding the image of her daughter in her mind's eye. In this vision Veda is sleeping, chin tucked, mouth slightly open, snoring gently but deeply enough that Sue can see the straps of her car seat tightening and loosening slightly across her daughter's chest. Marilyn sits beside her, awake, alert, ever vigilant. Sue embraces the image, coddles it. As if imagining Veda in her car seat might somehow preserve her, protect her.

Which she knows is patently ridiculous.

But Sue *also* knows with that same lead-pipe certainty that a certain amount of ridiculous faith in oneself must be waterproof, fireproof, and shockproof until it is impervious to doubt. For better or worse, she has learned two or three hard lessons about the depths of human depravity, probably knows more on the subject than anyone she's ever met. And the one thing she took from that experience in the summer of 1983 was that when there's blood on the line, whether it's your own or somebody else's, there is no room for self-doubt.

It's surely the reason why she got so bored in college and dropped out to become an EMT. Once you've been fire-baptized, you lose your taste for the milk and cookies of academic life.

And Sue thinks, here we go loop-de-loo, dovetailing into the central undercurrent of her life, something that a bald, pretentious little psychiatrist named Dr. Henry from Harvard Square had pointed out to her the one time she actually tried therapy. Dr. Henry's observation—put forward manfully enough considering that he was a short little clinician with a high-pitched voice and coffee breath—was that Sue Young has always related to the best things in her life neither through their presence nor their absence but their loss.

And not even bald, fat little Dr. Henry was fey or fussy enough to suggest that Sue Young's "innocence" might have been the first and most influential loss of her life, the one by which all other losses would be measured. But the idea had still sat there unspoken between them, session after session, staring at them like a lab rat chewing on a legal pad. Until the day that Sue walked in and handed his receptionist an envelope containing a letter that said, in essence, she was going to find another way to spend the hour from two to three on Thursday afternoons.

The sign up ahead reads: GRAY HAVEN—6.

Sue floors it.

GRAY HAVEN, the white sign says. ESTABLISHED 1802.

It is, as she remembers it, a muttered curse of a town. It has little to recommend it except that whatever else life has in store for you will be an improvement.

Sue hasn't been back here in almost fifteen years, since her mother died. The truth is she misses it like acne and braces.

Townsend Street, meanwhile, has not changed noticeably. The corner bar, the Blue Parrot Lounge, is still here with its single neon Budweiser sign sputtering in the window. There is a video store and a nail salon and the Exxon station. The textile mill where her dad put in thirty-two years is still down to her left, a series of boxlike buildings sloped awkwardly against one another's shoulders like a group of men who can't remember what they had in common except the mutual inability to stand without assistance. The streets and sidewalks are empty. The snow tumbles down, looped crosswise through the intersection in front of her. Narrow row houses with broken porch lights. Somebody's idea of the future, once upon a time.

Sue drives straight through. If she wanted to go back to the old place she would take a right on Crill Avenue and follow it three blocks east. There would be the yellow one-story house where her unemployed dad sat with the *Boston Herald* and his oxygen tank for the last six years of his life, hunting through the classified section with a ballpoint pen. When a "business opportunity" caught his eye he would draw boxes around the listing, over and over, until the ad would lift right out, to be deposited in a neatly stacked pile of similar gray rectangles to his right. Every night her mother threw the pile away. Every morning her father started a new stack.

Coming up on the right is Sheckard Park. The wind whips harder here, ramming its way down the hillside, blasting snow hard against the side of the Expedition. The swings and slide where she played as a child are still there, their steel framework submerged in drifts like the masts of some doomed polar expedition. In the middle of it stands a statue of a bald man in muttonchops and a long doctor's coat, holding a Bible and a bone-saw, gazing stoically off to the west. Sue knows the plaque underneath the statue identifies the man as Isaac Hamilton, but it doesn't say what he did to deserve to be immortalized for decades, maybe centuries, of having pigeons shit on his head. There's a fair amount of writing on the plaque, some kind of poem, she recalls vaguely, but she's not sure. Although she grew up less than a mile from here, Sue's never bothered to look it up.

Past the park the lights of town diminish to a dull, pale haze in her rearview mirror and in front of her are occasional farmhouses, bankrupt auto body shops with state inspection signs dangling by one corner, and miles of nearly uninterrupted darkness.

Two miles down the road she turns right onto Old Gorham Road. It is a long, dithering country lane whose sole defining characteristic seems to be its determination to continue sloping steadily downward. It forks twice, and both times Sue bears left, the second time onto a one-lane gravel road with no posted name. Here the pines are close enough that their needles hiss against her windows. The gravel is covered with half a foot of snow but the Expedition makes short work of it. America's upper class is nothing if not prepared for a little impromptu off-roading.

The road straightens out. Up ahead in the high beams she can begin to make out the old playground, two metal swing sets now devoid of swings and a rusty, slumping slide, all of it overgrown by weeds. Sue's not sure whether this land was owned by the township or simply abandoned here by some private landowner, but at one point it was the choice make-out spot for a generation of townies, and not long afterward, a favorite place for local kids to hang out, just far enough away to require bicycles and determination.

Beyond it is the bridge.

It's less than an eighth of a mile in the distance but

to Sue it seems a whole world away. Like the tired lit-tle cluster of playground equipment and the road leading up to it, the bridge has never had any name that she knows of nor has it needed one. It is a lonely, one-lane structure buried deep enough in the woods that the only people who could find it would have to know these dark back roads inside and out and thus have been searching for it specifically, or have stum-bled upon it completely by accident.

Underneath the bridge is an overgrown swamp, two square acres at least, where a creek once flowed, long since dead. In the shadow of those rotten tim-bers, sunken beneath the stench of decaying leaves and plant life from decades before she was born, was the spot where something happened back in the sum-mer of '83.

Sue feels her neck and back coiling forward as if somehow to muffle her accelerated heartbeat. Sud-denly her mouth is full of sour adrenaline, its mercury drip in the back of her throat.

There is a memory here, half-buried in the wintry hush of falling snow, a thing out of some child's nightmare that years ago somehow made the leap into the real world.

All at once her phone chirps.

A great flutter of muscle causes her arms to fly up sideways, her left hand whacking the door.

"Hello," she manages.

"You made it," the voice says, sounding low and insolent, urgent, making her think of phone sex. "I've been waiting."

Waiting. Sue stares out into the dark woods, her entire body momentarily reduced to what feels like an enormous pair of eyes, darting and searching the thick blackness piled in layers around her. "Are you out there?"

"What do you think?"

Sue is breathing through her mouth. Her heart goes *thump, thump.* She can hear herself, her body doing its job, keeping her brain alive. Something vaguely reassuring about the lumbering way that it goes about its work. Come hell or high water it's just another day at the cracker factory for the old human body.

He is out here too, somewhere. In the darkness, she thinks, very nearby. Perhaps under the bridge waiting for her or even closer. With the trees and the darkness and the snow, he could almost be close enough to touch.

"What do you want me to do?" she asks. She thinks reflexively of those girls in the 1-900 ads they run in the back of the *Boston Phoenix* and the comparison, though jarring, is not without validity. *Hi, my name's Sue. Tonight I'll do whatever you want. Just name it.* Sue can practically hear her friend Natalie rolling her eyes, saying, *Please,* but right now that's how the voice on the phone has made her feel. Tonight she is his fear whore.

"Stop the car and get out. Keep the phone with you."

Sue puts the Expedition in park and cuts the engine. Doing this she thinks only of Veda, but now apprehension for herself has joined her fear for her daughter. She opens the door and slides down and out into the cold air. Her jacket bunches up momentarily around her waist, allowing for the blade of the wind to graze her bare skin, and she shudders, an all-over tremble that spreads from her extremities inward to the base of her spine. Without thinking she puts on her gloves and stuffs her left hand in her pocket.

Her eyes water and her nose stings at the sharp temperature drop. Standing beside the car with the dome light on and the reassuring little chime of civilization reminding her that, whatever else is going on, the door is still ajar, she waits for the sensation to come back, the feeling of being watched.

She doesn't have to wait long. She feels his stare pressing down on her from somewhere close. It is horrible, this feeling. The fear sinks to the pit of her stomach.

"Get the shovel and the canvas out of the back," the voice on the phone says. "You'd better take the flashlight too. It's going to be very dark where you're going."

"What do you want me to do?"

"I want you to go down underneath the bridge."

"Is that where you are?" she blurts, although it's not actually what she means. What she means is, *Is that where my daughter is?* But these questions—and any others she might care to raise—are met with such total preemptive silence on the other end that Sue realizes that he's hung up again. And now she senses that there will be nothing more forthcoming until she does as she's told.

And of course there is another problem. The items he asked her to get out, the shovel and the canvas, are not in the Expedition. They are not in the Expedition because she didn't bring them. In the case of the canvas tarp, at least, the voice on the phone must know this, since he was the one who came and took the tarp from the garden shed himself.

She does however have the flashlight and for the moment the flashlight will have to do.

Now ankle-deep in snow, she begins edging her way toward the embankment, where the bridge takes over, with the phone in one hand and the flashlight in the other. Shining it under the sagging timbers she realizes immediately the light itself will do very little good since she has no idea how deep the snowdrifts are down there. On the third step her right foot plunges through the snow to her crotch, throwing her off balance, and for an ugly, dizzy moment she is sure she's going to go tumbling headfirst down the slope to land in a heap in the frozen swamp below.

Instead she grabs one of the timbers, hooks her left arm around it, and clings there for a span of seconds until her center of gravity is at least partially restored. Then, turning the edges of her feet against the angle of the hill, she inches downward once again, eyes riveted to the circle of the flashlight's beam ten feet in front of her. As she descends fully beneath the bridge the drifts taper away to wet, bare ground. No amount of wind could blow snow down at this angle.

Then the smell hits her, not incrementally but all at once.

The ripe and boggy rot panting upward from the very pores of the earth. It speaks directly to her limbic system and suddenly it is a long time ago and she and Phillip are standing down here, with pieces of hay and grass and sticks stuck to their skin, sweating and filthy among the clouds of gnats and mosquitoes. Staring at each other dead-eyed with the knowledge of what they've done and the work that is still ahead of them on that endlessly long afternoon.

You can't tell anybody, he tells her.

Sue nods at Phillip's ghost, his earnest, eleven-year-old face split down the middle by a single ray of sunlight falling from a crack in the bridge above their heads. A bird cries out with a cackling trill.

Now she is standing at the bottom of the hill. It is so dark down here that the very absence of light itself seems to swallow her up, consuming the flashlight's illumination in a single gulp. Still, if she looks out of the corner of her eye she can make out the rough outline of wooden piling twenty feet to her right, its base implanted crookedly in the dirt. There is no wind down here, but it is cold and damp.

Her cell phone rings in her hand. She touches the button to answer but doesn't say anything. For a moment neither does he.

"Are you in the place?"

Sue realizes she's just nodding. Clears her throat. "Yes."

"You're sure?"

"Positive."

There is silence again. Only this time she knows he

has not hung up. And not too far off in that impenetrable blackness Sue thinks she hears something moving beneath the bridge, a slow, moist rustle of motion against the clutter of decaying foliage. Something down here with her, moving steadily, unhurriedly in her direction. It might be a deer or some other kind of animal. It could be anything.

Abruptly she thinks of a line from another one of Veda's board books, *Bedtime Pets,* one line in particular that always struck her as a little sinister somehow.

Bedtime pets like children best, when the children are at rest. And when the children are asleep, bedtime pets come out to creep.

"Who are you?" she whispers into the phone.

The rustling sounds stop. Sue snaps her head around, breathing fast and hard. Blood pounds in her throat. It's almost painful.

Bedtime pets come out to creep.

The flesh up and down her back feels like it's going to leap right off her shoulders and run away.

And the voice on the phone says, "Start digging."

Sue makes her way over to the crooked wooden post. She stares at it. She says, "I don't have a shovel."

It's impossible to tell if the voice on the other end is still there or not.

"I didn't bring the shovel," she says a bit more forcefully. "I'm sorry. I left it—"

"Well then, you better do what you can with your hands," the voice cuts in. "Your little girl has less than ten hours to live. Do you understand that?"

Sue sets down the flashlight, props it up between two big stones so it's aimed at the post, and drops the phone in her pocket. It is time to get down to business. Dropping to a squat she sinks down to her knees, feels the moisture soak straight through the fabric of her pants to her skin, and leans forward.

She's almost forgotten that she's been wearing gloves this whole time, and as soon as she takes them off she starts to realize how bad, how truly awful, this is going to be. Her fingertips and knuckle joints immediately start throbbing with the cold. Still, she digs with her bare fingers into the slimy, clayey surface, prying up great slabs and clots of stinking, half-frozen muck and tossing it aside by the handful.

And she digs.

Time disappears. The only thing she has to compare it to is the three and a half hours she spent in labor with Veda, the epidural wearing off, the pain that could not get any worse, the hours that could not stretch any longer but somehow did. Phillip was there with her the whole time, Phillip who would be gone soon enough but for the time being was next to her bedside trying to help until she ordered him to stop telling her how to breathe.

And she digs on. Fingers long since numb, scraped so raw that when she finally does find it, it is the sound of the thing rattling against her hands, rather than the feel of it, that makes her realize she's dug it up.

The unmistakable synthetically slick surface of a familiar garbage bag, dirt-smeared and tattered, sits visibly in the cone of the flashlight beam. Several garbage bags, actually, taped in layers with packaging tape. And she remembers. Just the way they left him.

Tape it good, Sue, she hears Phillip saying, across the gulf of years. *He's got plenty of tape in here so just keep going.*

Sue sits upward, gulping air, and jerks erect so sharply that her backbone gives a sharp zing of pain. The world beneath the bridge reels in her peripheral vision. She is enduring equal portions of nausea, horror, and pain. But the thing she's unearthed, oblong and bulky, shrouded in garbage bags and bound up in packaging tape, tips the scale further toward horror—and the smell of it is beyond description. She vomits convulsively, twice, into the pile of earth she's pulled up.

Coughing, she wipes her lips and crawls back from it, not wanting to be any closer to the thing than she absolutely must be, for any longer than is absolutely required of her.

In her pocket the phone rings. She hits TALK.

"Are you finished digging?" he asks. "Did you find what I asked you to?"

"It's right here."

"Pick it up."

At first she can't believe she's hearing him right. "What?"

"You heard me."

"Why?"

"You're taking it back to the car."

"I can't. Do that."

He says nothing.

"I mean, I don't . . . why do you want me to take it to the car?" The feeling is creeping back into her fingers and by *feeling* she means pain, bright neon pain as if someone is crushing each fingertip between red-hot pliers. Faintly Sue is aware that at least one of her fingernails has torn almost completely off and there is blood trickling down between the webs of her fingers, the wound stinging with a crust of salty filth from the hole she dug. "I mean, haven't I done everything else you wanted up till now? I haven't called the police and I never tried to do anything except what you said." She waits, needing this to be acknowledged even as she knows that it won't be. "Can't you just let me have Veda back?"

Still no answer. Except this time Sue knows, somehow, that he is still there, listening, waiting. She can practically smell him through the cell phone, his breath not unlike the stench rolling off the thing in the garbage bags.

"I'll give her to you in the morning," he says with soft finality. "I'll give her to you in a little basket. And in another little basket I'll give you her heart. And another for her liver. And her kidneys. And two very small baskets for her pretty bright eyes. All wrapped up in ribbons. Would *that* be all right?"

"Stop. I'll do it. Whatever you want."

Now the slowness in his voice is the weariness of patience wearing thin. "I already told you that I'm a big believer in second chances, Susan. But I've given you enough of them already. We've got a long night ahead of us still and it's not even midnight yet. I'm starting to feel like you're taking advantage of my generosity." Now comes the other version of the voice, the one that hooks and peels back the layer of mock civility like a serrated knife, and Sue feels herself tensing against its edge. "I'm going to have to punish you, do you understand that?"

"Please just don't hurt Veda."

"I'm going to have to punish you," he repeats even more meticulously. "Now you do what I told you, pick it up and take it back to the car, or it's going to be even worse."

He hangs up, and Sue gives herself a second, literally, to try to pull herself together. Taking more time than that isn't going to do her any more good.

Hauling in a deep breath she drops down on her haunches in front of the thing wrapped up in garbage bags and forces herself to find some kind of grip on the shape within.

Something inside crackles and pulls loose with a sickening snap and a pop and she has to fight back the urge to throw up again. But she tugs once, twice, and again, and the thing comes loose from the sucking maw of the earth so abruptly that Sue falls backward. She has time to think, *This isn't going to happen,* and then it does, the thing in the bags falls on top of her, its unevenly distributed weight holding her down, seeming actually to almost grope for her, like it's trying to feel her up. A whiff of putrid air pours out of the bags and up into her nose.

Sue screams. She kicks and twists sideways, contorting her body to propel the thing off of her with a great uncoiling shudder. She wants to keep kicking it, shrieking at it, but already a degree of rationality has come back to her—again this is what she does, what she in fact *is,* an individual with the learned ability to find equilibrium in the most unlikely circumstances.

Sue takes another deep breath, bends down, and starts to drag the garbage-bag-enshrouded thing upward. It is lighter now, or feels lighter, no doubt because she is prepared for it. Rounded edges and jagged shapes press up against her chest and she is still distantly, unavoidably aware of the smell but a new kind of numbness has begun to take over for which she is nothing but grateful, grateful, grateful. In small, incrementally paced baby steps she drags the thing back up from underneath the bridge where she and Phillip buried it. Three-quarters of the way up she realizes that she left the flashlight down there and that she is now moving in almost total darkness, and this does not seem to matter to her much anymore either.

By the time she reaches the Expedition, she's sweating and badly winded, gasping for air. She drops the thing on the gravel road next to the rear tires and opens the back of the vehicle. The headlights and taillights have gone out now, but her eyes have adjusted. Sue bends down to grab the thing but its weight is too much for her fatigued muscles.

No way am I going to be able to lift this higher than my waist.

You have to.

She gives herself a ten count, as ready as she'll ever be, then sucks in a deep breath and leans down, gripping the shape with both arms. Straining with her arms, back, and shoulders, she hoists it upright. Something pops in her right knee. She can feel the vessels in her face and temples swelling with pressure. For one terrible moment she loses her balance and she and the thing in the garbage bags do an absurd little two-step around the back of the Expedition, staggering like a dance-hall girl and a cowboy too drunk to stand. Then she's back on the balls of her feet again, where her balance is, and she shoves the thing into the back of the car, then slams the door shut.

Not until she opens the driver's side door and climbs inside does she realize there is someone sitting in the passenger seat next to her.

And for the second time in ten minutes Sue Young screams.

As she screams, she scrambles backward away from it, half jumping and half falling back out, but her leg gets caught on the inside of the door and Sue gets one good look at the face staring blankly back at her from the other side.

It is Marilyn.

It is Marilyn the nanny.

Marilyn's body is very still and silent. Marilyn's hands lie on her lap. Marilyn's head is wrenched around sideways to face her. Marilyn's shoulder-length blond hair hangs damply over one side of her face. Marilyn's hair is red and stiff with blood like doll's hair. From outside looking in Sue sees the scooped-out sockets of her skull gape red and raw where her eyes once were. A sheet of paper has been stuck to the front of Marilyn's blouse with dried blood, and Sue can see a single word scrawled across it:

PUNISHED.

And once more the phone begins to ring.

S ue doesn't know how many times it rings before
she answers it.

"I told you you'd be punished."

"You didn't have to." Sue's voice is drab, lifeless. It
hangs in her throat like a tattered flag on a windless
day. "You don't have to do this."

"Don't beg. It's pathetic. And you're wasting t—"

"Who are you, you son of a bitch?" The words fly
out of her mouth before she can stop them, borne
along on a torrent of fury she never would've guessed
she had. *"If you've got something you want from me
why the fuck don't you come out and take it?"*

"Come out and take it?" The voice lets out a chuckle,
actually sounding appreciative. "Oh, I like that, Susan.
I like it a lot. I see you've grown some balls since we
talked last."

"Who is this?"

"You'll figure it out eventually. That's part of it
too." The voice gets nasty again. "Now get back in
the car. We've got some traveling to do tonight. Quite
a bit, actually."

Sue looks in at the corpse in the passenger seat staring back out at her. The lifeless thing that used to take care of her daughter, the friendly, slightly chubby girl who once nursed equal passions for Heath Ledger and Heath Bar Crunch and had been Veda's guardian and daytime companion for the last year and a half. The grief that she anticipates is still too deeply submersed in shock to make itself known.

"There's a blanket in the backseat," the voice says. "If you don't want to look at her like that. I wouldn't blame you. Death is pretty darn ugly, isn't it?"

"Fuck you."

"Fuck *me*? You're getting downright feisty, Susan. Maybe it's time for me to wake up your daughter so you can hear her scream again. What do you think?"

"No," Sue says, "no, no. I'm sorry. I won't—I shouldn't have said that." And despite what has just happened to Marilyn, right now all she feels is relief at the notion of Veda sound asleep through all of this. It is an irresistibly alluring thought.

"Get in the car."

Sue climbs in with the phone still pressed to her ear, takes the blanket from the backseat, and with her right hand spreads it clumsily over Marilyn's lap. Now she does cry a little bit, but silently, sparingly, like a few droplets of condensation leaking out from a high-pressure valve.

"Look at the note that I left you."

"I saw it."

"Look again."

Sue makes herself look at the bloody message stuck

to Marilyn's chest. The sheet of paper that it's written on is actually a map, and when she looks more closely she realizes that it's a map of eastern Massachusetts. It starts just west of Worcester and covers the state line right to the coast. The ragged edge of the map would seem to indicate that it had been torn out of a spiral-bound road atlas.

"What is this?"

"This is your route for the rest of the night," the voice says. "Are you ready to ride, Susan?"

S ue peels the map from Marilyn's chest and lays it on the dashboard. Above the word PUNISHED she can see that a route has been highlighted in careful yellow marker, the lines ruled into an up-and-down zigzag pattern across northern Massachusetts beneath the New Hampshire border.

On first glance the route defies logic. It is made up of a combination of country roads, grinding its way in a general northeastern direction from Gray Haven toward the coast. It is by no means direct—rather, it wobbles and bobs erratically through an apparently nonsensical symphony of detours, as if someone were following a bumblebee overland, back to its hive.

The only thing that lends any degree of order to the route is the string of small northern towns that it connects, none of them large enough to warrant red letters on the map. There are seven of these towns strung together by this jagged yellow NASDAQ line, starting with Gray Haven. From there the line meanders through communities named, in order from west to east: Winslow, Stoneview, Ashford, Wickham, and

East Newbury before ending at someplace called White's Cove, which perches on Cape Ann just west of Pigeon Cove.

Sue has never heard of any of these towns before, despite the fact that she's lived in Massachusetts most of her life. She certainly can't remember ever seeing any of them on a map. Of course there are literally hundreds of crappy little burgs scattered throughout New England that no amount of regional familiarity could possibly make her aware of, but it's somehow unsettling just the same.

Although let's face it, that might be due to the partially draped corpse of her nanny in the passenger seat, not to mention the stinking, Glad bag–draped thing stowed in the back.

"You've got your route laid out for you," the voice on the phone says. "You've got your cargo in the back and you've got nine hours of night left. If you get started now you should be back in White's Cove by seven thirty A.M. tomorrow."

Instinctively Sue's eyes go to the fuel gauge. Thank God she filled the tank after leaving work.

"Why do you want me to do this?"

"You'll figure it out as you go."

"What happens when I get to White's Cove?"

"You'll know by the time you get there."

"And that's when I get Veda back? Alive?"

"Always keep my promises, Susan."

Sue wishes that she could believe him. Right now she wishes it more than anything. "Where will she be?"

"The address is Eleven South Ocean Avenue. But

fair warning, Susan: If you come even one minute late—or if you get there using any other route but the one marked in this map—you can still have her back. The only difference is that she'll be dead. Do you understand the terms of this agreement?"

"Eleven South Ocean Avenue," Sue repeats, "White's Cove."

"Look for the statue."

"Statue?"

"And just a reminder in case you were thinking about somehow alerting the police—"

"How do I know you're telling the truth?"

"You don't."

Something happens in Sue's brain. A neurological event that she does not anticipate, a thing that begins where fear ends, a mother's outrage coupled with an ambulance driver's low-bullshit threshold. "All right." She is not yelling. She is being very quiet. "I'll do what you ask. I'll drive through these towns with this thing in back. I won't call the police or anybody else. I'll be there tomorrow morning to pick up my daughter. *But you listen to me.*" She pauses to take in a breath. It is a little disorienting to hear her voice sounding like this. As if some other persona has re-emerged from a few years of civility, affluence, and good manners to remind her that, at one point, she understood with adolescent ruthlessness that the world ran on blood. "If you kill my little girl tonight then you better make goddamn sure that you kill me as well. Because you're taking away everything I have in the world. And I will spend every waking moment for the rest of my life tracking you down. When I do, I promise you that you will die in a way so horrible that even a sick, sadistic son of a bitch like yourself would have to spend weeks trying to come up with something more painful than what I've got planned for you." She breathes. "Now do you understand *those* terms, you cocksucker, or do I have to make it clearer?"

It is a good moment—it almost makes her feel human again—but she is greeted with nothing but a puff of cottony silence from the phone and she knows that he has hung up on her yet again. At this precise instant, however, Sue Young does not care. There are welcome times when the truth spills out of our mouths because holding it back is like suicide. This is one of those times.

She puts the Expedition in drive and, gripping the map in her right hand, starts to turn around and head east.

Ten minutes later she is flying back through Gray Haven with her foot on the accelerator, the map on her lap. It's the kind of automotive sleepwalking that people do on the most familiar roads, the roads that carry them to their jobs, to school and church, the neighborhoods of their friends and family, back and forth through the towns they'll grow old and die in. The years she spent away from here might never have elapsed—she feels as if she knows every pothole and curve from Townsend Street to the outskirts of town.

She glances down at the map, at the route and the remaining six towns that lie ahead of her. Clearly they've been combined in this order for some reason, though any attempt to find logic in a system devised by a man who kidnaps infants and plucks the eyes out of their nannies is, to say the least, ill-advised.

Still, she goes over them in her mind, one at a time, seeing the names, trying to make them add up to something.

Gray Haven.

Winslow.

Stoneview.

Ashford.

Wickham.

East Newbury.

White's Cove.

Six towns she's never heard of and one she knows inside and out.

It doesn't make any sense.

Maybe it's not supposed to make any sense.

She's near the end of Townsend when another car pulls out of a side street in front of her. Sue hits the brakes. The Expedition goes into a skid, its back end coming around and finally stopping less than five feet from the other vehicle. Sue's heart stops.

It is the old farm pickup.

It sits perfectly still in front of her, its engine burbling, its headlights on. Before Sue has time to react the door opens and the driver jumps out.

This time he's standing directly in her headlights and she sees him clearly, the outline of his body as clear and bright as a life-size cardboard cutout of a pop star in a record store. But even so, the disconnect between what she's expecting and what her eyes actually report is surprising enough that it still takes the data a moment to percolate through her consciousness.

He's just a kid.

No, she thinks, not a true kid, but young and lean, late teens, with a long face, short-cropped hair, and no expression. His eyes are cups of shadow. He's wearing a T-shirt that hangs out over his jeans, and no jacket. And he's headed toward her.

Sue is still fumbling for the wheel even as he runs over to the Expedition and comes right up to the passenger side, yanks the handle, and opens the door. He actually tries to climb inside before realizing that there's something in the way.

"What the hell is this?" He's got a surprisingly deep voice for someone his size and age, and a big Adam's apple that goes up and down as he talks. He yanks the blanket off so Marilyn's face is exposed. "Holy shit!" He jumps backward, practically tripping over his own feet, and stares past Marilyn at Sue. "There's a dead girl with no eyes in your front seat!"

"Who are you?" Sue asks.

"There is a dead fucking girl with no eyes in your front seat!"

"That's my daughter's nanny, Marilyn," Sue says, and she sounds so calm saying it that she too is having some difficulty believing all of this is unfolding quite the way it seems to be. "You don't know anything about that?"

"It's already happening. Oh shit, I knew it, it's already too late." Now the kid is opening the door to the backseat, climbing into the Expedition on the right side behind Marilyn's body, and crouching down with his head low as if anticipating a mortar attack. "Come on, we've got to get out of here." This doesn't come off as a demand so much as a plea, as if he's on a mission as urgent as hers. "I'm serious, lady! Let's go!"

"Who are you?" she asks again.

"I'll tell you later, just hit it."

"Hold on," she says. "You've been following me. You're telling me that you don't have anything to do with my daughter's kidnapping?"

"Not me." The kid shakes his head and points. "Him."

Sue is about to turn around and ask the kid who he's talking about when she sees another car coming toward them from behind, rolling down the middle of the snowed-over road toward the pickup. She sees it clearly now. It's a van, the old-fashioned rectilinear model of no particular color.

"Who is that?" she asks.

"Look," the kid says, "I'm telling you for your own sake as well as mine, we've got to get out of here right now, okay? The dead travel fast. Just get us the fuck out of here."

"First tell me why you're following me."

"To *protect* you!" he explodes. "Now come on, let's go."

Sue puts the Expedition into drive and starts moving east down what's left of Townsend Street. At the same moment, on the other side of the street, the van is pulling up alongside the kid's pickup, where it creeps to a halt. She sees movement inside the van, dark and indiscriminate, and then they're too far away to see anything else.

"Who was in that van?" she asks, as Townsend Street trails away and becomes Route 117 in her rearview mirror. "Was that the man who kidnapped Veda?"

The kid crouched behind her in the backseat doesn't say anything. She can hear him breathing, cornered-animal style, and it sounds like he's trying to keep every nerve in his body from bursting through his skin all at once. Sue keeps her eyes on the road. She flashes back through everything that just happened and sees it all clearly, though it doesn't make any more sense than when it first happened. There's no question that the old farm truck was the same truck she saw out on the road an hour or so earlier, when she was first trying to dial Phillip's number in Malibu. It's the same truck that flagged her down after the night at the pumpkin patch. Probably the same truck that chased her out of the Prudential Center. And those are just the times she *noticed* it. So the kid has to be an integral part of it whether he admits it or not.

"Why did you run away the last time you saw me?" she asks.

No reply. Sue looks back. Then she sees the head-lights coming up behind them fast. Right away she knows it has to be the van.

It's approaching fast, and she doesn't see any partic-ular reason to try to outrun it, especially not with the roads the way they are. So she just lets it get up close behind her, until the kid cowering in her backseat re-alizes that it's there too and starts freaking out again.

"Wait a second, what are you doing?" he asks. "He's getting too close. He's going to see me."

"Then keep your head down," Sue says, and pulls the wheel hard to the right, giving the van plenty of room to pass. Sure enough, the van swings into the oncoming lane, right alongside them, and the kid in her backseat shuts up, ducking his head. Sue is aware of the looming dark shape of the van holding at fifty miles an hour to her immediate left. Then a flashlight beam sweeps out of the driver's side of the van, trained directly on Sue's face, and it's so bright that when she looks over she can't see anything but white light that makes her eyes ache.

"Don't look at him!" the kid's voice pipes up from behind her. "Don't let him see your face!"

For about half a second she considers hitting the brakes to get the light off her face and then disregards the idea—again, why bother? The van's driver apparently sees whatever he was looking for, a scared woman in her thirties with a dead body partially uncovered in the passenger seat, and the flashlight beam goes off, leaving spots flashing in Sue's eyes. The van's engine revs and it goes blasting up ahead of her, disappearing around the next curve.

"He's gone," she tells the kid. "You can come up now."

"He's not gone." He sits up, climbing and unfolding himself into the backseat right behind her head. "He's just playing with you."

"Who is he? Who are *you*?"

"My name's Jeff Tatum." He tosses it out there so offhandedly that it has to be the truth. "You don't know me. I live in Gray Haven."

"You've been following me for months." This is just a guess but she's pretty sure that if she's wrong, he'll tell her. "What do you want? How do you know me?"

Big surprise, the kid doesn't answer. Sue realizes that he's reached between the seats and grabbed the map with the route planned out on it. He stares at it. "Where did you get this?"

"It was stuck to Marilyn's body."

"Punished, what does that mean?"

"It means he was punishing me. Killing Marilyn and leaving her body here was my punishment. Why—"

"What did you do?"

She turns around, looks at him. "I'm done answering questions here. So far you haven't told me anything."

But Jeff Tatum is just staring at the map, reading the names of the towns aloud. "Winslow, Stoneview, Ashford, Wickham . . ." He jerks his head up at the road in front of them. "Whoa, wait a second. You're not actually *following* this route, are you?"

"Yes."

"Oh hell no. You can't. You can't do that."

He starts to crumple the map up and Sue grabs it back from him, stuffing it down between her knees, then turns around far enough to look him straight in the eyes. "Leave it alone. I don't know who you are or what you want but so far all I've seen you do is jump in my car and come unglued. It's been an insane night so far and unless you start telling me what you know about my daughter you're bouncing right out of here even faster than you came in, and I don't care who you're running from."

"Listen to me, Sue, Ms. Young, seriously—" The earnestness that comes into his voice now is almost as alarming as the fact that he knows her name. "I'm sorry about earlier, when I stopped you up the road. I figured that you were calling the police, or even worse, on the phone with him, and I knew if I tried to say anything to you, he'd hear me. I panicked and got back in the truck and drove away."

"Who is he?"

But Jeff Tatum is looking out the windshield at the road ahead. "I don't know what he told you about this route or these towns, or what you think you're doing, but this is really a huge mistake."

"Let me tell you what I know," she says. "I know that somebody kidnapped my daughter tonight. Whoever it is killed her nanny and he's given me orders to drive through these roads and these towns by tomorrow morning if I want to get her back. I don't know why he wants me to do it, and I don't care. All I know is that I'm driving his route."

Of course she's left out one small detail, the thing wrapped in garbage bags in the back of her car, the whole point of everything. And the kid seems to know it too. He doesn't say anything, but his eyes watch her in the rearview mirror, reminding her of how they gleamed from the truck's mirror earlier, only now they look softer, haunted by something deep inside.

"Why were you following me?" she asks.

"I already told you, to protect you." He sounds like he means it. "To protect you and your daughter and other people from getting killed."

"You're protecting me by stopping me from doing what this guy is telling me to do?"

"Exactly."

"That doesn't make any sense."

"If you know your history it does."

"History of what? People who do stupid things?"

"The history of murder in New England."

"And you know about this, why?"

"I've done research. I know this route. I know what it can do. Just trust me, okay, this is not something you want to mess around with."

That does it. Sue takes her foot off the gas, letting the Expedition roll to a gentle halt. Of course the kid notices this and pokes his head back up hopefully. "Wait, we're stopping?"

"Get out."

"Wait, you can't just leave me here."

"Believe me," Sue says, "I'd like to."

"I'm trying to help you."

Sue opens her door and climbs out into the cold stillness of the long, empty road in front of them. "Come on, let's go."

"What are you doing?"

"Rearranging a few things. You're sitting up front with me. And then you're going to tell me what I need to know." She looks him right in the eye. "I mean it."

11:39 P.M.

Their first job is hoisting Marilyn's body from the front seat and transferring it to the back. The kid holds Marilyn's legs and Sue takes her under the arms, with the nanny's head propped against her chest so it doesn't fall backward. For about two seconds Sue thinks this is going to be difficult for her emotionally, cradling the lifeless body of the woman who cared for her daughter, but she surprises herself with her own stoicism. Not that she doesn't love Marilyn like a little sister, not that the horror at what happened has diminished one iota. But these feelings have become remote, as if her heart's fallen asleep the way a leg or a foot might when circulation has been cut off.

The kid—well, the kid is a different story.

He tries to be a tough customer about it but when he gets back into the passenger seat next to Sue she can see how washed-out he looks, his face the color of the mushrooms that grow under the bridge in the summer, the slick nasty ones with spots on them. Mentally she's readjusted his age to seventeen at the outside. He keeps wiping his hands on his jeans and that Adam's apple of his just keeps bobbing and jerking like he's trying to swallow something greasy that he can't quite keep down.

"I shouldn't be up here. He might see me."

"You can crouch down if it makes you feel better," Sue says.

He tries. He's too tall. "Not all the way. There's nothing to hide behind."

"If the van comes you can jump into the backseat. But right now I want you up here. Now, fasten your seat belt." She hits the gas.

The kid grabs the dashboard. "Hold on, where are we going? We're not going to Winslow. I thought you were turning around."

"Winslow is exactly where we're going," she says, "and after that, the next town on that map, all the way through, until we get to what is it, White's Harbor?"

"White's Cove," the kid corrects her. "You have to remember that. From Ocean Street in old White's Cove, across the virgin land he drove . . ."

Sue feels something curdling inside her. She knows this tune or at least it's familiar to her from when she was young. "What is that?"

"It's an old poem," he says. "You have to remember it. It can help you."

"Help me how?"

"He hates the poem. They made it up a long time ago as a kind of charm to keep him away. It's like the only thing around that's as old as he is, so it's got some kind of power over him. Pushes him back inside

so that whatever he's infected has a chance to get out.
Maybe not for very long, just a few seconds, but hell,
sometimes that can make the difference, you know
what I mean?"

Sue just looks at him. "No."

"Just listen," he says, and in a slightly more audible
voice he begins to recite:

> *"From Ocean Street in old White's Cove*
> *Across the virgin land he drove*
> *To paint each town and hamlet red*
> *With the dying and the dead.*
> *He walked through Wickham and Newbury*
> *In Ashford or Stoneview he might tarry*
> *To call a child to his knee*
> *Where he slew it—One! Two! Three!*
> *Then from Winslow to Gray Haven*
> *Where he may begin again*
> *Bedecked in his unholy shroud*
> *To paint the Commonwealth with blood."*

"Who is *he*?" Sue asks.

"You don't know?" The kid looks at her, his eyes as
big as silver dollars. "Isaac Hamilton." Then some-
what bizarrely he reaches for the radio dial and seems
to remember it's not his. "You mind if I turn this on?"

"The radio? Why?"

"There's something I want to hear." Without waiting for express permission he hits the power switch.
Sue has it set for the Boston NPR affiliate, but the kid
thumbs the scan button up to 102.8 and sits back as

an obnoxious modern rock song, half-rap and half-screaming, plays through. Sue winces but doesn't say anything. She regards this music with the kind of irritation she reserves for mosquitoes and coffee shop hipsters who wear desert camouflage ironically.

Finally, as the DJ comes on, Sue looks back at the kid. "You know, I've still got a lot of questions for you."

"Shh." The kid cocks his head to the speaker, listening to the DJ's voice.

"You're listening to Damien on the midnight shift, WBTX, 102.8," the DJ says, "playing all your requests right on through till morning. Keep listening for more requests including one for that new War Pigs track and . . ." There's the sound of paper being flipped over and the DJ laughs. "Oh, I like this, Elton John's 'Daniel,' for my good buddy Jeff in Gray Haven."

Sue sees the kid nodding to himself. "Jeff in Gray Haven," she says. "Is he talking about you?"

"Yeah."

"You requested an Elton John song?"

He nods. When the DJ comes back he says, "Okay, Damien here on the X midnight shift and like I said, I had a request here from Jeff to play Elton John's 'Daniel.' Now, obviously this isn't the sort of thing we normally play here on the X but Jeff's what you might call a special case. Some of you might remember when he called in to the midnight shift last summer and told us how he lost his brother, who died a few years ago—the kid's name was Daniel." The DJ hesitates like he's not sure he wants to go into this, then plunges right in anyway. "And as we're on the air Jeff mentioned the Engineer."

Just like that, Sue's whole body goes cold. She looks at Jeff. "What is he—"

"Shh," Jeff hisses, staring at the radio dial.

"Now," the DJ continues, "I don't know if any of you were listening that night but if you were you know what I'm talking about, because we had some pretty messed-up people calling in to say some wild things. It turned into kind of a big deal, actually, the cops came by the station afterward and the whole thing was just totally out of control. Anyway, I'm just going to play the song, so here you go, Jeff."

The song starts, Elton John hitting those first few notes, and Sue sees the kid tilt his head forward toward the glowing dial. Two tear tracks shine down either side of his face, the kid crying silently in the dashboard light.

And Sue says, "What's the story with your brother?"

Jeff Tatum, monotone: "He died."

"What does the Engineer have to do with it?"

The kid doesn't say anything. He sniffles and wipes his eyes with the heels of his hands. Lets out a shaky breath. "The Engineer killed him."

"What? When was this?"

Jeff Tatum looks at her. "Three years ago."

"That's crazy." Sue feels herself go numb from the stomach outward. "That's not possible."

"That's what you think," he says, reaching into his pocket. "First, though, you better listen to this. I taped it last summer because I had a feeling he'd call in and I wanted to have proof." Without further explanation he pulls out a cassette tape from his hip pocket and pops it into the Expedition's tape deck. Static hisses and Sue hears the DJ's voice come on again, Damien, cut back in mid-sentence, saying, "listening to 102.8, the midnight shift, all-request line . . ."

Then her phone starts beeping.

Sue stabs the power on the cassette deck off and gropes down to answer the phone. "Yes."

"Hello, Susan," the voice says. "How's your passenger?"

She freezes. How would he know about Jeff? Had he seen Tatum come out of the truck? Was there some kind of bug in the Expedition? *Say something,* she commands herself. *Anything is better than just staying silent.* "I don't know what you're talking about."

"I hope you don't mind that I took out her eyes. Don't worry. They'll come back."

"Her . . ." Then Sue realizes that he's talking about Marilyn. "Her eyes."

"Oh yes. They are the windows of the soul, after all."

Sue doesn't answer. Her mouth feels sealed shut. Up ahead on the right side of the road she sees a white sign coming up. WINSLOW—ESTABLISHED 1802. The same year as Gray Haven.

"Susan, are you still there?"

"I'm here."

"That's good. So am I. I'm very close."

She frowns, leaning forward, squinting through the glass. There's a shape behind the sign. It's not hiding— it's much too big to hide behind such a small sign— but there is a sense of it *crouching* there, a shadow tensed to spring. Then Sue realizes what it is.

It's the van.

And there's something else too. In front of the van, all but invisible in the falling snow, the outline of a man stands motionless at the side of the road. All Sue can tell is that he's holding something in his hands. Then the headlights hit him and Sue sees a glimmer of something shiny. Teeth? Eyes? His face is blanched by the intensity of the lights. It's actually like he has no face. Then he's moving, taking five or six quick strides straight out until he's standing in the middle of the road ahead of them. Sue hears the kid in the passenger seat groan with terror.

"What was that, Susan?" the voice on the phone asks immediately.

"What was what?"

"That sound. Is there someone else there with you?"

"No." Sue has time to grab Jeff's shoulder, pushing him toward the floor and mouthing the words *get down.*

But he's not moving, his eyes locked on the figure in front of the van. Sue starts to turn the wheel. "Get down!" She feels the tires hiss and glide, losing their grip on the road. At last the kid seems to get it. He comes uncoiled all at once and starts to leap up between the passenger seat and the driver's seat, heading for the back. But his right leg catches on the lever for the emergency brake, his ankle twisting as he flails, kicks, trying to get free.

"Who's in the car with you, Susan?"

"Nobody, I told you, I'm alone."

"You lied to me."

"No, please." At the same time Sue is able to see with a kind of dismal clarity the figure in front of them raising the object in his hands. From twenty feet away she can tell that it's a rifle. The man in the road brings it up to shoulder level, tilts his head, and takes aim.

Sue's foot goes down hard on the brakes. Time seems to take in a deep breath and hold it as the Expedition throws itself into a spin, Sue floating underneath her seat belt, light and darkness flickering past her windshield like a dreaming eye.

There's the flat crack of a gunshot and a shout of

light as the Expedition's side window blows out with a crash. Next to her the kid howls. The car shoots through a crust of snow and grinds to a stop.

"Help me," the kid is saying in a watery voice, somewhere behind her head. "Please help me."

Sue sticks it in neutral, unfastens her seat belt, and starts to turn around. The kid's leg is still twisted between the seats but she can't see the rest of him down there in the dark. His breathing sounds like somebody blowing through a garden hose. On an unconscious level her brain is making assessments, ambulance driver assessments, and none of them are good. "Don't try to move. Are you hit?"

The kid doesn't say anything. He just makes that sound again.

She switches on the dome light and hears herself suck in a deep breath through her teeth. The kid is lying there looking up at her. The entire lower right side of his face has been obliterated, reduced to a lumpish mass of blood, muscle, and exposed bone. His right ear is gone and blood is pouring steadily down his neck from a hole in the side of his skull, the fresh blood steaming in the cold air that comes in through the shattered window. His eyes are dreamlike and moony, the lids fluttering.

He finally manages to speak, the words sounding like they're coming from the bottom of a bowl of extra-thick oatmeal. "Is it bad?"

"You're going to be all right. Just hold still."

"Is it bad?" he asks again, though he doesn't sound particularly alarmed. "It's bad, isn't it?" There's a wet puttering sound and that's when Sue sees the gash in his neck, blood bubbling up through it. "Oh man," the kid says weakly. "This sucks."

"Don't try to talk."

He mumbles something that she doesn't understand. Then he grabs her hand and squeezes it, and his eyes go up to her, becoming intensely, almost preternaturally bright, making one last effort at communication. "I've been trying to contact you. I'm sorry. I waited too long."

"Take it easy."

"Kept backing off, when I thought I saw him."

"It's okay."

"That time downtown, I almost caught up to you, but backed away at the last minute. He knows me. Thought I saw him in the crowd. Couldn't take any chances. Afraid he might be using me to find you."

"Jeff," she says, with infinite tenderness, "the Engineer's dead."

"Not the Engineer." He coughs, struggles to swallow, his throat making that same thick bubbling noise. "See, it's not the Engineer, not really. It's Isaac Hamilton. He's . . ."

The bubbling noise stops. The kid's eyes glaze. It's not a dramatic thing but Sue has seen it enough times to know what it means. She doesn't have to check his pulse but she picks up his wrist anyway and waits a long moment before laying it down again. There are now three dead bodies in the car with her and two of them were people she's spoken to within the last few hours. For all she knows her daughter is already dead as well. There is no reasonable explanation for this except that she is caught in a nightmare. But it is not the kind of nightmare she will awaken from unless her definition of *awakening* is *losing her mind*.

On the other side of the windshield, something hits the hood of the Expedition with a thump. Sue's skeleton jerks inside her and she turns around to look. Beyond the windshield, standing on her hood, she sees a pair of leather boots.

She looks up, but can't see above his knees. The roof is blocking the rest of his body. The only other part of him she can see is the bottom of his long coat flapping at his legs. He's so close to her that she can see the color of the coat, dark green with a red flannel lining. Sitting here mesmerized she can literally count the buttons holding the lining into place.

BLAM!

Sue leaps, ears ringing, the gunshot coming from the roof of the Expedition above her head. Before she can tense up it happens again.

BLAM!

On reflex—at the moment, she has nothing else left in her arsenal—she throws the car into drive and hits the accelerator. The Expedition lurches to life. Something bumps off the roof and the man on her hood is gone. Sue takes the wheel and steers it back onto the road, looking in the rearview mirror but not seeing anything back there. He's just gone. The road ahead of her leading into Winslow is empty.

She drives fifty yards up the road, her stomach twisted backward on itself, the faint lights of Winslow beginning to prism in her eyes. When the road gets too blurry to drive she stops again, crosses her arms over her chest, and for a long time she just sits there holding on to herself and trembling. The dome light is still on and when she reaches around to switch it off with a clumsy, shock-stiffened arm she notices the kid sprawled across the backseat.

There are two bullet holes through the kid's eyes. Wisps of smoke are still floating from the sockets. Sue sees this but it doesn't register with her immediately. She is filled with the simultaneous urges to scream, throw up, and squeeze her own eyes shut—

But she sublimates all of these urges, puts them aside, with the single thought of Veda waiting for her at the end of the line. Veda the punctuation mark, the only good reason, the final and absolute meaning in her otherwise iffy existence. Veda, whom she is prepared to kill for, whom she'll die trying to get back. The simplicity of the thought steels her, helps her focus, until it is the only thing she knows.

Veda.

Baby.

I'm coming. Mommy's coming. I promise.

And she drives the rest of the way into Winslow.

12:06 A.M.

Winslow is only marginally less depressing than Gray Haven. It's deserted here as well, the sidewalks lit by occasional streetlights so she can see empty storefronts along with a barbershop and a boarded-up Depression-era movie theater called the Bijou. A dilapidated church made of fieldstone rises above the square. The local bar on the corner is the Crow's Tap and there is indeed a sign above the door with a picture of a crow tapping its beak against a keg. But if there's anyone getting a nightcap inside, they're doing it in the dark. Not the faintest trace of light trickles through the bar's front window. There are no footprints in the blanket of snow that lies across the town, no trace of life anywhere. And like Gray Haven, Winslow seems to be a town inhabited only by bad memories and worse weather.

A speed limit sign commands her to slow to 25 and Sue automatically lifts her foot from the pedal, not wanting to get pulled over by the town's one cop. Considering her current cargo of corpses, a routine speeding violation would turn into tomorrow's *USA*

Today headline for the deputy lucky enough to stumble across it. She isn't really thinking about any of this—in her current frame of numbness it would be a mistake to say that she's technically *thinking* about anything at all—but she knows if she gets stopped that she will never see her daughter again. This again is nightmare logic, but it is logic just the same. It is the kind of blessed circular logic, beloved of zealots and extremists everywhere, that means she doesn't have to think about it anymore beyond that.

But the doubts remain.

What if I do start thinking about it right now? The dead bodies, the kidnapping, the route, the voice on the phone—will I go crazy? Will my brain just throw up its hands and say That's it, I quit? Exactly how much horror and shock is the mind capable of absorbing, really?

She pushes it away.

At twenty-five miles an hour Main Street seems to go on forever. She speeds up, risking thirty-five, then forty. Despite the wind blowing in through the broken window, she's flushed, her cheeks and earlobes burning. She feels hot and dizzy, as if she has the flu.

Her eyes dart out the windows. She tries to pay attention to the town, to figure out why the voice would be so insistent that she detour through here on her way east. But there's nothing to see. She passes a gun shop, a creepily deserted hobby store called Pastimes on the Square, some cheap housing waiting to be bulldozed, a vacant lot, and at the top of the next hill, a barren-looking little park with a statue of a man standing on a pedestal.

He's bald with muttonchops, dressed in a long coat, holding the familiar bone-saw in his right hand as he gazes off to the west.

It looks just like the figure that stands in Sheckard Park in Gray Haven. Isaac Hamilton, the name that the kid mentioned to her.

However, there's one slight difference—this version of the statue has only one arm.

It's odd enough for Sue to look twice, sure she's just seeing it at a peculiar angle, but no, the arm is gone. The left one, to be exact, the one that was holding the Bible back in Gray Haven, is missing from the shoulder. Sue has no idea why two towns would have the same historic figure immortalized in their parks, and right now she couldn't care. Except that Isaac Hamilton is linked to the towns, and the kid linked Isaac Hamilton to the Engineer . . . all of which brings her one step closer to understanding the man who kidnapped her daughter.

Then again the kid also said that the Engineer murdered his brother three years ago, which Sue knows is flatly impossible.

She passes the statue and sees the entire village green is full of little statues, and realizes it's not a park at all. It's a cemetery. It spreads its old, flat, bald stones out across the snowy field like candy that somebody's sucked the letters off of, and she starts to hear the poem echo through her head, the one that starts "From Ocean Street in old White's Cove." All at once, boom, the headache that she felt between her eyes comes back. It's not a flu feeling anymore, it's more like a low-pressure system moving in. The dizziness in her head turns to nausea. Something else is different too, an odd crawling twinge in her chest and abdomen that she can't quite pinpoint.

Sue floors the accelerator and speeds up as if she could leave the words and feelings behind her, but the cemetery keeps going and so does the poem in her head. She's out of breath, her lungs feeling too small to deliver air. Her head is pounding. What is it about these towns, this route, and, as the kid said, the history of murder in New England?

She's almost past the cemetery when she hears a muffled scratching coming from underneath the dashboard to her right. It's mixed in with a sliding sound, like something is trying to drag itself up a vertical surface and keeps falling. Sue follows the noise down to the cardboard box with the two steamed lobsters that Sean Flaherty gave her, six hours ago.

The box has started shifting from side to side.

Sue stares at it. The lobsters inside are dead, of course. They've been dead ever since the good people at Legal Seafood dropped them in a pot for Sean at five this afternoon.

Inside the box the scraping grows more animated. She can hear clicking sounds too, quick angry snaps, along with the scuttling of many legs.

Phillip's voice says it first.

They're alive again.

"Lazarus lobsters," Sue says, almost sounding like her old self. "Jesus lobsters, Elvis lobsters."

She rolls down her window. There's a cardboard handle on top of the box and she's going to pitch the entire thing out the window. Then she's not going to think about it anymore, just like she's not going to think about the bodies in the back of her car or the song that tells her about the history of murder in New England. In fact she's going to restrict her thoughts to Veda and how she's going to be with her in the morning as long as she does what the voice tells her. Because this is what people do when they're dealing with maniacs. They do what the voice on the phone tells them.

She reaches down for the box, her fingers starting to curl around the handle, lifting it tentatively from the floor, when a boiled red claw bursts up from a flap in the cardboard. The claw is wide open, and it snaps shut on her hand, trapping the fourth and fifth fingers. Sue shouts in pain and surprise, jerks her hand back, yanking the entire lobster out of the box with it. It's shockingly big—two and a half pounds, Sean told her, though it feels a lot heavier dangling off her hand. But that's a lot less shocking than the fact that it's whipping around, alive and completely pissed off.

She's forgotten all about the steering wheel. The Expedition veers right and then weaves sharply left, comes inches from hitting the stone fence alongside the road until Sue swings the wheel back to the center again.

The lobster holds on to her hand even as she shakes

it, swings it out the open window, the thing dangling next to her face with its tail and legs clicking and snapping against the glass. Sue hits the power window, raising it so it catches the unprotected joint between the leg and claw and cuts right through it. The body of the lobster drops, leaving only the claw still gripping her fingers.

Holding the wheel steady with her knee, Sue pries the claw off, lowers the window again, and throws it out. Her hand is bleeding where the claw broke the skin, and between the pain and the cold, her arm is throbbing right up to the elbow. She presses her hand under her armpit and holds it there.

She sees that the graveyard is gone, taking the town with it, and she's back in open country again. The snow has tapered off to reveal a clear black sky. Keeping the window down, she inhales until her sinuses start to sting. The air smells clean.

She looks down on the floor, sees the empty box resting on its side, and remembers the second lobster. It's nowhere to be seen. She shuts the window next to her head and tries to listen over the whine of the wind coming through the shattered glass on the passenger's side. After a moment she hears it rustling under her seat, followed by silence. Without hesitating she leans forward and shoves her hand directly underneath her and grabs the lobster by the tail, pulling it out.

It starts wiggling. With strength that surprises even her, Sue slams it straight down on the dashboard with enough force to crack the plastic. The lobster's entire carapace explodes and sprays meat along with shards of shell and warm, salty water across her face and lap. She flings the thing's carcass across the passenger seat and out the broken window.

She gets out the map again and draws a line to the next town, measuring the distance at two finger-widths. According to the map's legend that means that Stoneview is about fifteen miles from here. She consciously tries to recall the poem that the kid recited to her, the one that she was terribly certain she could speak word for word only a few minutes earlier.

Now she can't even remember the first line.

12:39 A.M.

Following the capillary bed of secondary roads outlined on the map, Sue finds herself headed down yet another nameless stretch of blacktop. It's empty, but it's been plowed recently, and she's able to cruise along at a bracing seventy with decent visibility. Once again the mindlessness of driving becomes a tonic. There's no sign of the van or any other traffic. There is nothing but darkness and the broken yellow line receding in her headlights.

She's ten miles from Stoneview when her phone starts beeping.

For the first time she's seized by the inexplicable compulsion not to answer it. She knows that it's him, the voice of the man who has her daughter, and she has to answer. Still she lets it ring half a dozen times before finally forcing her hand to pick it up and hit the TALK button.

"Hello?"

The voice is right there in her ear, a moist, heavy murmur.

"Susan, are you beginning to understand what's happening here?"

"What?"

"The changes. Do you feel the changes?"

"What changes?"

The voice sighs. "That's what I was afraid of. You need to be punished again, Susan. It will open your eyes."

"No, wait." *No more punishment,* she wants to cry. "What do you want? Just tell me."

"I want to see you."

"What?"

"I want to look at you, Susan. I want you to look at yourself."

"How . . . ?" she starts.

"When you get to Stoneview, there's a place called Babe's. You'll find it."

"Please, don't—" she stops herself, realizing that he is still listening and probably enjoying hearing her beg, maybe that's the whole point to begin with. So instead she says, "Who was Isaac Hamilton?"

"Ah." He sounds pleased. "You *are* beginning to understand. Just when I was ready to throw you to the wolves."

"Is his statue in all the towns along the route?"

"Do you want to see your little girl in the morning, Susan?"

"Yes."

"Babe's, Susan. I'll see you there."

He hangs up before she can say anything else.

She puts the phone down, still cruising along at seventy, seventy-five. She doesn't know what else to do except follow the map. She thinks about Isaac Hamilton. The name has an enchantment on it. It has a kind of power, like a key dangling from a chain, a key that might open a box—or a cage.

Sure enough, six miles later, she sees the sign coming up:

STONEVIEW—ESTABLISHED 1802

The town is a husk.

Empty buildings with no glass in the windows, a dead gas station, vacant houses, and great dinosaur spines of snow drifted up in the streets. It's like a hurricane came through, or a virus, and took everyone with it. She wouldn't have thought such towns even existed in Massachusetts. And apparently they don't, at least on any map but this one.

Sue drives through it, her sinuses expanding, the enormous, cabbage-size pain at the base of her skull beginning to pound again. She feels a twinge of nausea, and her skin is moist to the touch. Her ribs squeeze her chest like a pair of skeletal hands. The lines and edges of the Expedition are running together— the bloodstains and bodies that she shouldn't be able to see are trickling into her peripheral vision, occluding her eyes.

Up ahead the road bends to the right, around an island of snow-buried land that she assumes was once Stoneview's town common. There is a bench, two or three bare trees, and in the middle, there is another statue. She says his name aloud.

"Isaac Hamilton."

As her headlights reach out to touch it Sue can see the statue plainly. And it's different again. This time it's just a head, body, and legs. Both arms are missing.

Now she slows down, magnetized. There's a small amount of snow on it but she can still tell right away, the arms were never there. It's not like a bunch of kids came along and cut them off as a prank or ran their car into it and knocked the arms off. The sculptor deliberately left them off, fashioning smooth stumps at either shoulder. Beneath the statue, the pedestal has the same plaque as the others, and Sue thinks of the lines inscribed upon it, lines that she never bothered to read though, somehow, she'd always thought they were poetry, by virtue of the way they were laid out.

She thinks of the poem that Jeff quoted. She squints at the old copperplate type—difficult enough to read already, abraded further by the passing decades. Though it's impossible to tell without getting out of her car (she's not getting out of her car, not here, not now, no sir), she thinks it looks long enough to be the poem.

So what? So they wrote some poem about Hamilton, so what is that supposed to mean?

Her eyes shift away. Behind the statue the road rises and falls again. Instead of a cemetery, the hill behind the statue gives way to an unexpected surge of red neon, a glowing cigarette tip aimed at the flat, windowless structure cowering beneath it like a blind dog.

Babe's is a roadhouse surrounded with crookedly parked vehicles. Travelers like herself, Sue thinks, caught in the storm. She pulls in and cuts the engine. Already she can hear the music playing inside, a machinelike thud of pure distortion, skinned of all melody. Bending forward to climb out triggers something in her stomach and she almost gets sick, managing to hold it back at the last second.

The cell rings.

"I'm here," she says.

"I see that."

Sue stops and turns around, her eyes searching the lot until she sees what she's looking for. The van sits shivering in a handicapped spot with a rag of exhaust dangling from its tailpipe. She can see nothing inside.

"What am I doing here?"

"I'll let you know when the time comes," the voice says. "Go around to the back. Go through the kitchen. Inside you'll find another door, marked Employees Only. Go through it. And keep that phone handy."

She starts walking. There's a freshly shoveled pathway leading around the side of the building and Sue follows it until she hears voices murmuring quietly in Spanish or perhaps Portuguese, she can't tell. There's a light mounted on the roof, aimed down, and a giant fan blasts the smell of fried onions mixed with garbage and cooking grease. Two men in aprons and bandannas are passing a joint back and forth behind the Dumpster. They flick their eyes up at her for the briefest of appraisals and then resume their conversation.

Sue passes them on the way to the door, a featureless steel plate propped open by a plastic yellow mop bucket. She slips inside without touching it and finds herself in a filthy kitchen. The music that she heard outside is louder back here, bouncing off the dirty tiles and pans dangling over the stove, and she can hear men's voices shouting and whistling on the far side of a pair of swinging doors. A roach scuttles across the sink and disappears under a bag of frozen chicken wings.

She puts her shoulder to the doors but they won't budge. There is another door off to her left, marked EMPLOYEES ONLY, a strange sign to post inside the kitchen. Sue turns the handle and steps into a dark dressing room that smells like perfume and sweat. It's shaped like a railroad car with a long counter covered in Kleenex wads and jars of cotton balls and makeup kits. There's just one light, a dim lamp without a shade burning in the corner, the wattage so low that it hardly casts a shadow.

On the far side of the room a red curtain hangs and the roar coming from the other side is somehow bestial and benign at the same time, like a crowd at a ballgame. Suddenly she understands that the place isn't called Babe's but Babes, and what the voice on the phone expects her to do here at one in the morning.

"Where are you now?" the voice asks.

"I'm in the room."

"Take off your clothes."

"What?"

"You heard me."

I want to look at you. I want you to look at yourself.

Sue doesn't move.

"Take off your clothes and I'll let you see Veda. She's right on the other side of that curtain." It's not clear whether the voice is teasing her or not. "You do believe me, don't you, Susan?"

In the end it doesn't really matter. Laying the cell phone faceup on the counter next to a jar of nail polish, Sue takes off her bloody coat and drops it on the back of a chair. Then she unbuttons her blouse. There's a lot of blood on it too and more on her skirt, making the fabric stiff and tacky as it slithers off her hips—funny how she only notices that as she's taking it off. She unhooks her bra and peels off her underwear, letting it drop to the dirty floor where it lies like a dead jellyfish among the footprints and cigarette butts.

Naked, she's neither hot nor cold, the thermostat in the room being perfectly adjusted for nakedness, but that's not the first thing she thinks. The first thing she thinks is how infrequently she's taken off her clothes without a mirror, as if for some reason she needs one to get undressed, the way you need a mirror to put on makeup or fix your hair. She's always watched herself undress, she realizes. Whether it's in the bedroom or bathroom or a dressing room at Bloomingdale's, her stare has always inevitably found its way to the glassy rectangle reflecting the white cave-drawing of scars that crisscrosses her stomach and slashes over her breast to puncture and divide her right nipple.

But there aren't any mirrors in this changing room, an odd thing to leave out. But then, why would a stripper need a mirror when it's only skin she's presenting?

She picks the phone back up, holds it to her ear. "All right."

"Now step through the curtain."

Sue does. The curtain slides off her arm and her bare thigh and she's standing out on a stage with a white spotlight blasting her in the face. She can hear a zoo of men whistling and cheering at her. Sue squints into the light and it's like staring right at the sun. She can only make out the vague shapes of tables with men at them, and the music, tribal and deep, pouring out of speakers that surround her head. Her eyeballs vibrate in their sockets. The music somehow seems to be making it harder to see.

Looking behind her Sue sees another woman standing next to her, arms hanging at her sides. The stripper looks pale and awkward, with wild eyes and a drugged-out whorish expression, a zombie fucked back to life. But she's so raunchily gorgeous standing there, so exotically out of her mind that despite everything Sue finds herself staring at her until she realizes it's her own reflection.

The back of the stage is a giant mirror.

Only the woman in the mirror doesn't have any scars on her belly or her breast.

She looks down. Sue doesn't have those scars anymore either.

She doesn't have her scars anymore either.

Slowly she runs her fingertips down over the smooth terrain of her stomach, then back up over her newly restored nipple. The crowd, taking it for showmanship, screams gleefully back in encouragement.

The spotlight leaves her and sweeps through them, picking out clusters of wide-eyed, openmouthed faces like a sniper from a tree. One by one the faces fall away from the light. They scream and vanish, scream and vanish.

The light keeps sweeping.

Sue stares at it, following it with her eyes.

Then in the front row Sue glimpses Veda.

S itting in the yellow-and-blue stroller that Marilyn keeps in the Jeep, Sue's daughter is pale and motionless, her eyes closed, mouth slightly ajar. The stroller is parked between two tables of people. And the girl is still, so still.

Without thinking Sue jumps off the stage. It's farther down than it looks and she lands hard on her heels, twisting a tendon in her right ankle with a twang that she can feel. She ignores it.

She reaches for Veda and starts to pull her up, but her daughter is fastened into the stroller. Veda's warm body struggles fitfully and Sue realizes that she's *moving,* thank you, God, she was only asleep but now she's moving as Sue fumbles with the first of two plastic latches that hold the canvas restraints in place. Sue's hands are trembling, her heart hammering spastically against her sternum the way that it never did on the job, because this isn't like saving someone else's life, this is like saving her own life—she's a rookie at this.

The spotlight swoops away, burying them in darkness, and then circles back again, only now it's pulsing across the entire room, making everything happen in a broken, jumpy necklace of images. Sue continues groping for the second latch, feeling her daughter's body stiffen and stretch as Veda opens her eyes, looking drowsily up at Sue with a moment of dawning recognition and relief, and Sue can see her daughter's lips drawing together to form the word *Mama*. Somebody shoves Sue sideways, something sharp catching her in the ribs, an elbow, and she's sprawling naked, her bare ass skidding on the floor, legs and arms knocking over chairs and a table as she tries to scramble back to her feet. The crowd screams louder. Through the tables she sees a group of three or four people drawing together around the stroller, closing it off from her, the small white oval of Veda's outstretched palm reaching out between their bodies before it disappears in a forest of legs.

Sue screams her daughter's name and throws herself among them like she's digging a grave with her bare hands. She clutches skin and fabric and hair, yanking out clots and patches and chunks. It all comes to a halt with a fist flying into her face, a white flashbulb between her eyes that sends her crashing backward again. Sue spills like a bucket of water and somebody catches her under the arms, now she's being dragged away, her bare heels squeaking along the sticky floor, until she feels a gust of cold air across her belly and they're spinning her, throwing her out.

She feels wet pavement against her lips, smells garbage, beer, onions, tobacco, grease.

Rolls on her back. Opens her eyes.

Next to the Dumpster, the two dishwashers she saw earlier are gazing down at her, the orange firefly of the joint's tip floating back and forth to illuminate first one face and then the other. At last one of them leans down to offer her his hand. They continue to stare as she rises to her feet.

"You okay?"

"My daughter," Sue hears herself say. Her lips feel two syllables behind the words they're emitting. "Her name is Veda Young. She's been kidnapped by some people in there."

They blink at her, so stoned. "Ki'nap?"

"They're in a van. It's parked out front. They've been following me all night to make sure I do what they want. They've got my little girl and they told me if I . . ."

One of the men unclips a cell phone from his apron string and holds it out to her. "You call police?" His dark eyes watch her closely.

Sue takes the cell phone. She looks at the man's face. His eyes are black and reflect no light. There is nothing there that she can see, either way. "Is there a pay phone anywhere around here?"

"Pay phone?"

Then behind them in the parking lot something slides into view, moving steadily across the snow. Her eyes fly to it, already knowing what it is. The van. For the first time she realizes that it's gray, the color of brain and ash, as if by default.

It stops forty feet away, turns away from her, and sits, waiting. Thirty-eight feet closer the two men continue to stare at her body. They've given up offering their assistance and have gone on to simply ogle her bare breasts and the glossy blue shadow of her pubic hair. Over their shoulders Sue sees the back of the van open. She steps around them, toward it. There's a long pause and then something falls out of the van with a clank.

It's the stroller. It lands on its front tires, teeters briefly, and then tilts forward and collapses so that the bundled shape inside, a soft pellet refusing geometry, vanishes underneath it.

Still naked, she breaks into a run.

Closing in, the van starts moving again, Sue tasting carbon monoxide in its wake. Her feet, numb as beef, smear crosswise over a patch of packed ice and disappear beneath her. Just before she starts to fall, she grabs the stroller, which flips over sideways with the force of her tackle so the handle hits her in the face. What spills out is a bundle, a canvas-wrapped package, and as Sue pulls it out she realizes it holds a coat. There's something soft buried in its folds.

Not a child.

Clothes.

They spill like entrails across the snow. Not the ones she left behind but clean, unfamiliar ones, a pair of sweatpants, underwear, a T-shirt and turtleneck sweater, socks, gloves, and a bra. Nondescript wool coat with a hood. Two boots. Something slides out of them.

A cell phone.

It begins to ring.

"So now you see," the voice says. "You see *your-self*."

It's a few minutes later. Sue has climbed back inside the Expedition, wrestling the newfound sweatpants up around her hips. This is difficult enough, holding her hips off the seat by pressing both feet to the floorboard between the gas and the brake, but at the same time she has to keep the cell phone clenched between her shoulder and her jaw. The clothes are too large for her, the sleeves of the sweater flopping over her hands, the sweatpants bagging slightly around the ankles—nothing fits, and the footwear he left for her is a pair of men's snowmobile boots. But at least they're warm. She's got the engine running and the heat on, combating a chill seeping in from the broken window.

Outside, cars are pulling away from Babes, leaving the parking lot, shuffling home through the blizzard. Closing time.

"My scars," Sue says. "What happened to them?"

"What?" he asks.

"The scars from my accident." Once again she runs her fingers over herself and once again she finds the scar tissue missing, supposedly permanent geography erased by an unexpected reversal of time's current. How easily things enter and exit a map. "They're gone."

"You're a smart lady, Susan, you figure it out. Think hard."

"It's like they've been healed."

"Healed?" He sounds disappointed. "That's a meaningless term in this context. You were an EMT for enough years. You know you can't heal something that's already dead."

Meaning her scars, she thinks, dead tissue.

"What about the lobsters?" she says. "I had lobsters in the car. They were boiled, completely dead. But while I was driving, they . . ." Feeling him waiting, she makes herself say it. "They came back to life."

"Ah."

"But that's not possible."

"There are two kinds of people in the world, Susan. Pragmatists like yourself, who believe what they see, and the rest of the world who, when they see something they don't believe or can't understand, pretend that it isn't there. You've seen these things, and felt them for yourself. So why are you fighting it?"

"It can't be real."

"Oh, but it is real. It's as real as the knife I'm holding to your daughter's throat. And believe me when I say, the longer you wrestle with this, the closer the knife gets."

That punctures the moment for her. She doesn't have to think about it for long before it hits her that this was one of the reasons he chose her. Besides digging up the thing underneath the bridge, she was also, as the voice on the phone said, a pragmatist, one who could be counted on to believe what's in front of her no matter how impossible it seems. So she says exactly what he wants to hear.

"This route," she says, "and these seven towns. When you drive through them in the right order, it brings the dead back to life."

"Bravo."

"But why—"

"Now do you understand the significance of what I'm asking you to do?"

Automatically: "Yes."

"No," he says, "you don't, not yet. But you will."

No, she thinks. All she really understands is that she saw Veda again, touched her and almost got her back. Then she failed. Also she understands that her night is not over—there are hours left until daybreak—and after what she's just done she has no idea what else to expect between now and then.

"Don't worry, Susan. Veda's still safe and sound for the next five hours. She's sleeping. She never saw her mommy standing naked onstage in front of strangers."

He hangs up.

A red light appears in the corner of her eye.

She looks down.

On the dashboard she sees a diagonal blip the size of a fingernail clipping which, along with that chiming sound, is indicating that one of the doors is ajar, specifically the passenger door behind her on the right.

Opening her door, she steps out, walks back to pull the other door open the rest of the way with the intention of slamming it shut. That's when she sees it.

Jeff Tatum's body is missing.

The leather upholstery in the backseat is still looped and spat on with his blood—otherwise the fact that there isn't another corpse back here might never have struck her as noteworthy—but the body itself is definitely not present.

She peers behind the seat, into the storage space where Marilyn's body still rests next to the thing wrapped in garbage bags, with Sean Flaherty's case of booze crammed between them like some kind of sick joke. She doesn't know why she checks back there, it's not like the kid was in any shape to climb over a seat. And he isn't there either. He's gone.

Turning around slowly, Sue looks back at the parking lot, deserted now except for one or two cars parked off in the distance. Snow keeps falling, covering them up. It is so silent that she thinks she can hear the far-off buzz of the light behind the building. There are no traffic noises, no other sounds at all except for her breathing. Her eyes shift reluctantly forward.

There are marks in the snow, leading away from the passenger side of the Expedition. Long, scraping tracks with red streaks down their centers. The marks shuffle away from her in sequence, creeping upward from the vehicle in the general direction of the embankment dividing the parking lot from the main road. Sue's eyes trace them. Midway up the embankment she sees the heap of rags that can only be the kid's body.

She walks over to it.

Tatum's corpse is sprawled on its belly, his buttocks humped in the air, the back of his skull torn open so she can see the cavern where his brains lived until the man standing on her roof blew the kid's eyeballs through them. One arm sticks out while the other is folded beneath him.

If somebody dragged the body out of her car, why would they just leave it here? And if somebody *didn't* drag it out . . . ?

From here Sue can see that there's something tucked under the body, a sheet of paper. If it's what she thinks it is, she needs it back.

Squatting down, she reaches out for the triangular edge, tugging the corner of it out from beneath the weight of his chest—and just as she thought, it is the map, the one with the route outlined on it, the one that says PUNISHED. Whoever dragged the kid's body out here brought the map along too, maybe as a message, maybe as something else. It doesn't matter. All Sue knows is that she needs that map to get her daughter back, and she's certainly not going to leave it out here in the snow just because somebody left a dead body on top of it.

She starts to pull it the rest of the way out.

The corpse rolls over, its arms shooting out for her. Too startled to shout, Sue lets out a gasp and falls hard on her side on the embankment next to the body. The map lands in the snow next to her. She's not so much frozen as paralyzed, all her muscles disconnected from her nerves. The kid jumps on top of her, the raw, black-red holes of his eye sockets facing her straight on. There's something shimmering deep inside the sockets. They don't quite look like eyes. Sue doesn't know *what* they are.

"Please," she says.

The sound of her voice is all he needs. He lunges for her. She feels only the faintest pressure as his fingers dig into her neck, but she sees him and hears him, smells him even, with exaggerated clarity. His face is the color of yogurt that's been left out of the refrigerator too long. What's left of his jaw goes up and down and makes a dislocated clicking noise and she can see his tongue flickering around inside his mouth. Their faces are so close that Sue smells cordite floating from the ruined crockery of his skull along with the sourness of scorched tissue. He pushes the words up out of himself, snatching the map back, wrinkling it, and shoving it in her face.

"Don't go . . ."

His breath steams faintly in the night air, less so than her own, his voice sounding like a cartoon version of the voice that's been talking to her on the cell phone.

"Any farther . . ."

A rotten sound pushed through moist ground beef.

"Up the road."

Paralysis shatters. Sue plants her foot on his chest and propels him back into the snow, the kid's legs tangling and bringing him down in a sliding heap. Sue rolls, rights herself, and grabs the map, backing away, putting as much distance as she can between herself and him, expecting him to jump up again and charge her.

But he just lands on his back. The initial burst of aggression seems to have cost all his energy, and his mostly empty eye sockets appear to have rendered him largely blind. Still on the retreat, Sue jams the map back in her pocket and watches him trying to roll over, reminded of when Veda was learning to turn herself on her side, no coordination and very little strength. One hand jerks and collapses across his face so he's talking into the crook of his arm. He's still trying to say something but she can't understand any of it now—it's drunk talk, random babble giving way to a ragged kind of sobbing, then spasmodic breathing, and finally silence. He twitches his right foot and falls totally flat and unmoving.

Stumbling back from the corpse Sue feels her way to the Expedition. She doesn't take her eyes off the kid's body, even for one second. This is only partly a matter of not letting her guard down. She realizes that she's hoping that if she looks at it long enough then she'll believe it. *Pragmatists like yourself believe what they see.*

At the moment her rather permissive ability to believe feels like a snake trying to swallow a pig. No matter how detached she is from the events of this night, no matter how far the elastic of her incredulity may stretch—and tonight it has stretched pretty fucking far—she cannot make herself believe that she just saw the kid's dead body sit up and attack her.

But it did. This is Phillip's voice in her head now, calm and steady. *And those scars on your body are gone. You're not waking up from this one, Sue. You need to accept that.*

Maybe, she thinks, maybe not. Phillip isn't exactly the go-to guy when it comes to acceptance.

She wedges herself back into the Expedition, still watching the body. It hasn't budged. Inside she hears the putter of paper rolling out of her fax machine. The cell phone is ringing too. She answers it.

"You found Tatum," the voice says. "Now you understand a little better."

"Yes." Telling him what he wants to hear. "A little."

"Good. Because it's important you understand your role in it."

"My role?"

"You're not just a chauffeur tonight, Susan."

She waits, her mind flashing to Gray Haven and the poem that Jeff Tatum recited and the statues of Isaac Hamilton. "What really happened in these towns?"

"You'll see when you're ready." The voice wants to change the subject. "Your fax machine went off. Who faxed you?"

"How'd you—" Sue starts to ask, but realizes he probably heard it in the background. She doubts he'll explain himself anyway.

She glances at the rolled sheets of paper tumbling over the passenger seat. It's the corrected bank agreement for tomorrow's meeting about Sean's pub space. Without looking at it too closely she guesses that Brad has gone through and anticipated her questions, marking the places where he needs her signature. Burning the midnight oil, making sure she's got a hard copy waiting in her car for the morning meeting, and none of it could matter less to her right now.

"It's a contract for a meeting," she says. "My office manager wants me to fax him back."

"You know the rules, Susan. No outgoing calls, including faxes."

"If I don't reply he'll suspect something."

"It's two in the morning, Susan. I doubt that."

She gathers the papers up in her fist. Even if she were going to try and fax Brad some distress signal, what would she write? *Veda kidnapped by a person in a gray van?* She doesn't even know the license number. And while she's not convinced that following the orders will get her daughter back, she's certain that disobeying them will get Veda killed. It's like faith but the opposite, a kind of sacred terror.

"Ashford," the voice says. "Forty-one miles. It's a long drive. Better get started."

She puts the Expedition into drive. Backing up, her headlights catch the patch of snow where the kid's body still lies, faceup. Even from here she can tell he's dead, something in the angle of his head.

Sue pulls the map out of her pocket. She settles it on her lap again and pulls out of the parking lot.

One last glance into her rearview as she pulls away. The kid's body is gone.

2:26 A.M.

Following the map, Sue heads southeast through the night. The road has no name. The only reason she knows it's the right road is that periodically, when it flattens and straightens and the snow isn't falling too hard, she'll catch a glimpse of the van's taillights up in the distance. She likes seeing the taillights because she knows that Veda is in there. And she knows it's the van because once she got close enough to see its dented back door staring back at her like an ugly face.

Then the van speeds up and she can't see the taillights at all.

She hits the gas, taking it up to seventy, then eighty, waiting for them to appear. Visibility isn't an issue at the moment but she still sees nothing. Maybe the van turned off and now they're behind her. She checks the rearview. Nothing back there. Not only are there no other cars on this route, there aren't any signs—no billboards, speed limit signs, or mile markers, just the endless pipeline of the night.

She finds herself thinking about the route, what it's

done, and the two bodies in the back of the Expedition. If it's true that driving through these back roads can resurrect the dead, then what about Marilyn? What about the other, the thing she dug up under the bridge?

She tilts the mirror down and turns on the dome light. She can't see beyond the backseat, nor can she hear anything over the sound of the engine and the tires on the road. But if a hand were to reach up over the seat, followed by the body itself slinking into the dark space behind her, she could see that. If she were looking, that is. If she weren't looking, or listening, she might not hear it until one of those cold hands slipped between the two front seats and clamped over her mouth. And then she'd hear the voice, right next to her ear. Would it ask her to take it farther down the road, she wonders. Or would it say something else, maybe some old poem about a man who traveled from White's Cove to Gray Haven, to paint the Commonwealth with blood?

She decides to keep the light on for now.

She drives another fifteen miles, watching for the next sign that will indicate her turn for Ashford. It's harder to see with the interior light on, but she leaves it on just the same. She remembers how Phillip always hated driving with the light on. Whenever they went anywhere, he would drive and she would navigate, and she always thought it was less about the light and more about her insistence on consulting a map as they went. If it were up to him, he would've found his way by sense of smell.

Why couldn't you be here now to help me get through this?

At some point she finds herself thinking about him in a deeper sense, and his sudden departure a year and a half earlier, the way he walked out of her life with almost no warning, leaving the details to his attorneys and accountants. In the brief and awkward telephone conversations that Sue's had with Phillip since then—the last one was several months ago—he always said that he wasn't ready for the obligations of parenthood, that he was afraid he'd be a bad father. For a long time Sue refused to accept that.

"That's your *excuse?*" she asked, during a particularly awful phone call last August, to which he replied, "It's my reason, Sue. And it's better this way. You'll just have to take my word for it." He refused to go into it any further than that. Ultimately it became easier just to believe him. Her husband, despite the fact that he always seemed like a stand-up guy, had run away from his life with her and Veda simply because he didn't think he was up to the challenge.

But what if he was running from something else? Something he couldn't possibly tell her about, for her own protection? And what if whatever it was caught up with him, within the last two months, and that was why the phone calls finally stopped?

She's still wondering about that when, behind her and approaching quickly, the blue-and-red police lights begin to flash.

"Ma'am?" The approaching officer is medium height, with a Jersey accent and tired eyes. He holds the flashlight up next to his head, shining it low enough that it doesn't blind her. The name on his tag reads O'DONNELL. Sue can see his partner sitting in the cruiser, and hears the dispatcher's voice on the radio. "Are you having car trouble?"

Sue stands next to the Expedition, staring back at him, not answering. Her fear levels are still off the chart and she's afraid that if she opens her mouth she might start screaming. And she won't be able to stop.

"Ma'am?" Now the flashlight goes into her eyes and she hears the cop's voice grow more concerned. "Is something wrong?"

No. No. Just say the word. Send him on his way.

Sue's head goes forward, mouth twitching. It probably looks like she's about to throw up. The cop stands there waiting until she finally gets the words out.

"I'm f-fine."

He shines the light on the Expedition, across its tires and license plate. "No trouble with your vehicle?

What are you doing out here in the middle of the night?"

"I didn't—" Her voice sounds strained and awful. She clears her throat, swallows and tries again. "I thought I saw something run across the road in front of me." She sounds a little better now, clearer if not steadier. "It was a deer or something, I swerved so I wouldn't hit it."

The cop shines the light on her tire tracks, running smooth and straight to the shoulder. Then back to her face again. "Where are you headed?"

"Ashford."

"Are you aware that there's a winter storm warning in effect for this area for the next twelve hours? You're not supposed to be on the roads unless it's absolutely necessary."

"It's an emergency."

"What happened?"

"Excuse me?"

"What kind of emergency is it?"

She stares directly into the flashlight beam, beginning to feel a balloon of apprehension inflating within her. "My daughter. She's—she may be in trouble. She's with her father. I got a phone call asking me to come pick her up. He told me to take this route. I'm not from around here." She's aware that her voice is rising in pitch as she talks, becoming shrill, but she can't do anything about it. "I mean, I am, but not this immediate area, so I was following the directions he gave me. I just have to get to Ashford."

The light leaves her face. There's a pause. She realizes that he's looking at her hands, bare and encrusted with dirt and dried blood from digging. He shines his light on the Expedition's broken window. His voice becomes formal again. "May I see your license and registration?"

He waits a good ten feet behind the Expedition while she goes back through the passenger's side to take them out of the glove compartment, all the while anticipating the noise or movement that will make him shine his flashlight through one of the windows. But nothing moves or shifts and he just stands back there, waiting. When she brings him her license and registration, he takes them from her.

"Return to your vehicle."

Sue goes back to the Expedition, opens the driver's side, and gets in, eyes riveted to the rearview. She can see both cops clearly inside the car, one of them talking on the radio, the other typing on the dash-mounted keyboard.

Sue stares at the phone, waiting for it to ring. It doesn't. Her eyes go to the wadded-up fax pages accumulated across the floor, a small pile of discarded paper, the detritus of her night thus far. The phone remains silent.

But in her mind she can hear the voice telling her not to say or do anything that might jeopardize Veda. It gets tangled up with Phillip's voice, the two of them merging into one, telling her to stay calm. She supposes this is the point, the voice eventually infecting her head so thoroughly that it doesn't need to call her anymore, it's just there.

At last the officer comes back with her paperwork, but he doesn't hand it back to her yet. He shines the light on her face again, not speaking for a long moment. "Ms. Young, are you sure there's nothing you want to tell me?"

She shakes her head. "I don't think so."

He leans forward. There's no expression in his eyes, but they are green and alert, and they seem kind as well, waiting for some sign from her, any indication of distress. "There's nothing I can do for you?"

"No, thank you."

He sighs. "All right. I'm going to . . ." Then, almost as an afterthought, he shines the flashlight into the back of the Expedition, Sue's eyes traveling with it to the still-bright bloodstains all over the backseat, the kid's blood sprayed everywhere like modern art. The cop instinctively takes a step back, face stiffening, the flashlight in Sue's eyes again, his voice cold and abrupt.

"Ma'am, step out of the car and keep your hands where I can see them."

3:27 A.M.

Sue steps out of the car again and sees the cop signaling his partner without taking his eyes off her. A moment later the other cop is out with his flashlight aimed into the Expedition, following the bloodstains across the upholstery.

"Ma'am, what happened here?"

"The deer, when I hit it . . ." She falters and gives up, unable to weave even the most rudimentary strands of the story together. "Please, can't you just let me go? I have to get my daughter."

Neither of them answers her. The first cop circles around the back and Sue sees him shining a light down inside, then opening the door. There's a rustle of blankets being pulled aside. Then an awful, staring silence.

"Jesus H. Christ."

The second cop, standing in front of her, reacts immediately to the alarm in his partner's voice, glancing over his shoulder. "Rich? What's going on?"

"Cuff her."

The second cop frowns, straining to see beyond the bloodstained backseat without turning completely away from Sue. "What is it? What's back there?"

"Cuff her, cuff her now!"

The urgency in his voice is contagious and for an instant Sue is irrationally compelled to make a run for it, jump back in the Expedition and go screaming off into the night. Of course this is idiotic, only morons try to outrun cops, and morons with dead bodies in the back *never* get away. Besides, the second cop is already turning her around, pulling her arms together, tightening cold steel at her wrists. He leads her around the back of the Expedition and Sue watches him join his partner, both of them shining their lights down on Marilyn's corpse sprawled on its back, mouth open, eyeless sockets facing up.

"Holy fuck."

"Yeah."

"Holy *fuck*."

Without speaking another word to Sue, the second cop takes her back to the cruiser. Inside it's warm and smells like coffee. She steals a glimpse at the dashboard clock, feeling the minutes flash by. She tries not to think about this but knows she can't help it. Where has the time gone? The night which just moments ago seemed endless is already draining away from her at an alarming speed, and Veda is that much closer to dying.

Eventually another cruiser pulls up, along with an ambulance and a tow truck. An unmarked sedan is the last car to arrive and she sees an older man with a beard step out, wearing a parka and holding a cup of coffee. He talks to the cops, looks in the back of the Expedition, then glances in Sue's direction. She watches as he scratches his beard and gets back in his car. The tow truck driver hooks the Expedition to the winch, and the others all return to their cars. The whole process takes a little over twenty minutes.

The sedan leads the procession back to town, followed by the ambulance, the other cruiser, and the tow truck hauling the Expedition. The two cops and Sue bring up the rear. They drive in silence for several minutes until, up ahead, Sue sees the sign along the side of the road:

ASHFORD
ESTABLISHED 1802

They drive past the sign, the road winding lazily into town. Unlike the other towns on the route, Ashford is still populated. The windows have glass in them. The streetlights work. The houses and shops along its main drag are dark, of course, but neon shines down from either side—shoe repairs and tanning salons—and the roads have been cleared recently. Two churches stand guard on either side of the main intersection, glowering down at the local Blockbuster. There's a park up ahead and Sue sees the statue exactly where she expects it, the man on his pedestal, except this time the figure is not only missing both arms, he's also minus a leg. He holds his head cocked proudly, like some flightless seabird.

"Isaac Hamilton," she says.

The cop behind the wheel looks back at her. "What?"

"That's him, isn't it?"

Neither of them replies, and that's all right. At this point she takes nothing for granted. As they roll through town she begins to feel something, light-headedness along with a flutter of nausea, and waits to see if it's going to get worse. But within seconds it's gone again. It's almost like a kind of mountain sickness, as if the air is thinner here but her body is learning to adapt more swiftly each time she passes through it.

At the Ashford Police Station the tow truck pulls her car around to the impound lot and the cruiser parks in front. The cops lead her up the steps and inside, bypassing the officer behind the booking desk, who buzzes them through. There's a TV and VCR under the desk, and Sue sees the booking sergeant is watching an old Clint Eastwood movie with the sound turned down. To her right she spots a bulletin board full of missing children posters.

They take her down a long white hallway that looks like it was recently constructed, past several darkened cubicles with computer monitors playing screensavers. At the end of the hall one of the cops opens a door for her, takes off her handcuffs, and ushers her inside, closing the door and locking it from the outside. Sue looks at her watch.

It's already four in the morning.

Veda, I've still got so far to go.

She looks around. The room is nothing but four white walls and a table with two chairs. She hears the climate control hum to life, pumping warm air into the room. It's already too hot in here. From the other side of the door she hears voices but can't tell what they're saying. Then it opens and the man with the beard walks in carrying a Styrofoam cup of coffee. Up close he looks even older than she thought, late sixties, past retirement age, dressed in a wrinkled white oxford with an ink stain on the breast pocket. He's got wintry gray eyes, caved-in cheeks, and the beginning of a gut sloping over his belt, and smells like cigarettes. He motions for her to sit and then sinks into the chair across from her and frowns.

"I'm Detective Yates, Ms. Young. We found the second body in your car. Want to tell me what's going on, or do you just want to call your lawyer?"

"You have to let me go."

He looks at her, raises an eyebrow.

"I can't—" She stops. He actually seems to be paying very close attention to what she's about to say and it makes it that much harder to talk. "There's no time to explain. If you let me go, I promise, I'll do whatever you want. I just have to get Veda back by tomorrow morning."

"Veda is your daughter?"

"She's been kidnapped. The kidnappers gave me very specific instructions." She waits for him to interject with a question but he waits her out with that same one-eyebrow-raised expression. "There was a dead body, the one in garbage bags. I had to go dig it up."

"From a grave?"

"No. It was buried under a bridge, back in Gray Haven."

Yates flinches at the name of the town. "And these kidnappers told you where to find it?"

For a half second Sue hesitates, not so much because she wants to tell him the truth but simply because it almost slips out on its own. Then she nods. "They told me on the phone that I needed to go get it and drive it through this route, and when I got there they'd give me my little girl back."

He wrinkles up his eyes at her. "When was all this?"

"Earlier tonight."

"And you didn't call the police?"

"He said not to."

Yates doesn't move, doesn't even look at her, processing all of this.

"What about the other body, the girl?"

"She's my nanny. They killed her after they kidnapped Veda, then they brought her body back and put it in my car." She forces herself to look into the impenetrable frown cut into the detective's face. "Look, I know how it sounds, but if I don't do exactly what they tell me, they'll kill her."

Yates looks at her for a while longer and stands up. He appears smaller now, shrunken. Something's been taken away from him. "Have you seen his face, any kind of a vehicle, anything like that?"

"It's a gray van. I don't know the license plate number."

He nods, once. "I'll be back."

"Wait, you can't leave me—"

The door swings shut and locks. Sue sits there and waits. And waits.

Ten minutes later Yates returns, smelling freshly of cigarettes. He's carrying something in a transparent evidence bag and drops it on the table in front of Sue. She instantly recognizes it as the map with the route highlighted and the word PUNISHED scrawled across the top.

"Where did you get this?" he asks.

"They gave it to me. It's my route. The kidnappers, they left it with Marilyn's body."

He puts his elbows on the table and rubs his temples. In the fluorescent lights his skin appears almost blue, the fine veins beneath it darker still. "Tell me, Ms. Young." His fingertips tremble as he turns the map around to look at it. "Are you from Massachusetts originally?"

"Yes."

"Do you know about the Engineer?"

"What's this got to do with . . . ?"

"Just answer the question."

Sue gazes at him flatly, this tired-looking stranger with the gray seen-it-all eyes. Once again she feels the impulse to tell him everything. It would be so much easier, telling the truth to someone, and he already thinks she's crazy so why not give him the whole story? But again some mental circuit breaker clicks into place and she catches herself, holding back. Whether or not this decision is common sense or self-defense or simple instinct is not clear to her. At this point her motives—beyond the obvious one to get her daughter back safely by sunrise—are nebulous to her. But she holds back just the same.

"Of course I've heard of him. I was a teenager when it happened. I remember seeing it on the news and hearing my parents talk about it." She shakes her head. "But I don't understand how that's got anything to do with me or my daughter."

Yates holds up two long fingers, like he's ordering a couple drinks. Sue notices that his nails are yellow and in need of trimming—bachelor's nails, she thinks. "There are two reasons I bring it up. First, as you probably remember, in the summer of 1983, the murderer that they called the Engineer abducted and killed thirteen children. Second . . ." He points at the map in the baggie. "This is the exact route that he traveled, east to west, through these seven towns, beginning June 12, 1983, in White's Cove and ending with the disappearance of the last child on August 22 in Gray Haven. So what's the connection?"

"I don't know," she says. "Honestly. I have no idea."

Yates frowns at her, obviously not buying this. But there's something else in his expression besides incredulity, something both simpler and more complex, and Sue sees it. She sees it in the mesh of wrinkles around his eyes and the eyes themselves, the way they've fastened themselves to her. It's like a hunger, a fever to find out.

She thinks about what he said, about the Engineer, the ease with which he reeled off the specifics of the case, the exact number of children and the precise dates. Despite his disclaimers and the affectation of uncertainty Yates has linked the route to the Engineer, at least to his own satisfaction. Going over these things in her mind it occurs to her that he might have his own connection to what happened that summer, just as she does. "Did you investigate the disappearances here?" she asks.

Yates's eyes flash to her. "Not officially, no."

Sue blinks. The answer doesn't make sense. Then she realizes it's because it's only half the answer. And the rest of it hits her with the clarity of winter light.

"Your child," she says, "was one of his victims."

Yates's silence confirms more than any words. All at once Sue feels a connection to the tired old man across the table. They've both lost a child—permanently in Yates's case, more immediately in her own—to a force that they're both still struggling to comprehend. It explains why a detective in his late sixties would refuse to retire, she thinks, just as it explains the unhealthy intensity burning behind his weary face. Out of the blue she thinks this cannot be a coincidence. Not because someone planned it: How could they? But simply because she is on the route, and there is something about this combination of back roads and towns, something ancient and frightening and explicitly unreal, wherein certain connections happen because they must.

"Her name was Rebecca," Yates says finally, the name seeming to take everything from him as he speaks it. "She was eleven years old that summer. That was almost his cutoff, you know. He never killed anyone older than twelve."

"I'm so sorry."

Again he doesn't seem to hear. "I'll never forget how my wife sounded when she called me at work that afternoon to tell me she was missing. It didn't even sound like her." Yates is shaking his head slowly, not looking at Sue, not looking at anything, really. This featureless, white-walled room is perfect for that. "Then three days later some hikers found Rebecca just outside of town. Most of her, anyway. He'd shot out her eyes, like he did with all the others." He pauses for a fraction of a second. "Like the body of the woman we found in your car, your nanny. And do you know the worst part?"

She waits.

"After we buried her? Someone dug her up. They dug up her coffin and took my daughter's body. Since then I've discovered that that's what happened to a lot of the kids from that summer. Nobody knows where they went, they're just gone."

Sue just nods. She's thought all of this already. Then the question pops out of her mouth before she even knows it's there. "Who was Isaac Hamilton?"

Yates—if it's possible—becomes even paler than before. "Isaac Hamilton?"

"The name on the statue, the one with one leg and no arms."

"Who told you about him?"

"Nobody. His statue's in every town along the route, starting with Gray Haven, and each time he's missing another extremity. Does that have anything to do with the Engineer?"

"No," Yates says definitively, but his eyes have wandered away from her. Then, in a softer voice: "Not unless you believe in a lot of superstitious bullshit."

"What kind of superstitious bullshit?"

"That's not important right now."

"I think it is."

Yates sighs. "We spent a long time following up the idea that the Engineer was somehow influenced by Isaac Hamilton. There's obviously a connection: the Engineer only killed children in towns where Hamilton's statue was erected, and Hamilton himself was a historic child-murderer, two hundred years ago. Even now there are a lot of nuts out there who think that . . ."

"Think what?"

"Who seem to think that Hamilton was controlling the Engineer from beyond the grave," Yates says. He does a pretty good job of keeping the inflection from his voice, all things considered. "Putting voices in his head or something. They come out of the woodwork with these theories, thinking that local police, state troopers, and the FBI haven't noticed the connection.

But frankly we're a little hesitant to accept that the Engineer was only a tool for Isaac Hamilton's eternal evil."

"How come I never heard any of this before?" Sue asks.

"You wouldn't," Yates says, "unless you were an avid reader of the *National Enquirer* and the *Weekly World News*. The mainstream media couldn't do much with it, except to make the comparison and let it drift. The supermarket tabloids, though, had a field day."

Sue opens her mouth to say something and snaps it shut again. The words she was about to speak, and whatever happened to them before they reached her lips, have eluded her entirely now, leaving a mortal coldness in their wake. Somewhere in the police station, a drawer slams shut, and she jumps so suddenly it hurts.

Yates clears his throat, sounding like he could use another cigarette.

"We don't traffic in horror stories and speculation, Ms. Young, we deal in facts, and in this case, the facts are pretty plain. There were two dead bodies in your car and a lot of unanswered questions. You'll forgive me if I'm not completely convinced you're telling me the truth about why you're involved in all this. You have to realize you're only hurting yourself by holding back. Why would whoever kidnapped your daughter want you to go and dig up a body, and then place another body in your car?"

Sue feels her voice slipping a bit. "I told you, I don't

know. All I know is that my daughter's in danger, she's going to die in three hours if I don't do exactly what they told me, and we're wasting time sitting here talking about it."

"We'll do absolutely everything we can to get your daughter back—"

"That's not enough." She's on her feet now, though she doesn't remember standing up, and she's practically yelling. "What if it were your daughter and you had another chance to save her, what would you do?"

"It *isn't* me," Yates says, not sounding particularly offended by her outburst. If anything his voice, his whole demeanor, has softened, become more sympathetic. "It *isn't* me, Ms. Young."

"But if it were? Wouldn't you do whatever it took to get her back safely?"

Yates, to his credit, seems to weigh the question seriously. "If it were my daughter? My Rebecca?"

"Yes."

"I never would've let them bring me in. I would've driven *over* those two officers before I let them stop me from doing what I had to do."

She nods, wearily. Getting him to admit this doesn't make her feel any better. It only makes things worse.

"But you *did* let them take you in," Yates says, "and now you're here. And regardless of how I might feel about the matter personally, it's my job to make sure you stay here until some of these questions are answered. I'm sorry. If you want to make a phone call, you're entitled to one." He too stands up, makes an oddly gentle lifting motion with his palm; it is an invitation, she realizes, to make the call. Sue goes to the door, and Yates taps on it once. Another police officer's face appears outside, an absurdly young-looking man with the wispy beginnings of a blond mustache, as the door swings open so Yates can guide her to the phone mounted on the wall. He gets a line out and hands her the receiver.

Sue dials the first number that comes to mind, her attorney David Feldman, and gets his answering service. She leaves the number at the station and hangs up, then lets them take her back to her little white room. She half expects Yates to follow her in, but he only gives her a nod and says he'll be right back.

The door closes; the door locks.

Sue sits and stares at it, trying not to think of the minutes as they dribble past. She starts to visualize Veda in the dark interior of the van and deliberately snaps the thought off. She can see her daughter just as clearly as before, but it no longer provides even the most fleeting succor. *Dear God, get me out of here.*

Ten minutes later she hears the screams.

4:41 A.M.

They coincide with a series of slamming sounds, like kitchen cupboards banging shut. The silence that comes afterward is seamless. After a span of seconds it's interrupted by a distant but distinct tumbling noise, something falling down heavily—it's *got* to be heavy if Sue can hear it here, at the end of the hallway. Then from somewhere in the guts of the police station she hears a man's voice yell: *"Holy shit!"* There are two more flat bangs. Then nothing. No bangs, no shouting. Not breathing, Sue moves toward the door, almost reaches it, and stops short.

From up the hall someone has begun to shriek, *"Oh God, oh Christ, please, please . . ."* It's so frantic that Sue can't even tell if it's a man or a woman. The screaming comes in jagged, irregular bursts, then goes so high that it becomes screeching, a mangled combination of pain and what she can only imagine is hysterical terror. The screamer actually sounds like someone going insane with fright.

Sue feels herself floating back from the door, its rectangular frame seeming to recede away from her, rather than staying in one place while she moves. She listens as the screaming intensifies, getting louder, closer, until it's right outside the locked door, wholly incoherent. Now it's accompanied by pounding, hands slapping against the door, clawing at the handle, rattling it with a desperation that makes Sue feel nauseated with dread.

There are two more flat cracking sounds. Gunshots, she realizes. The door shakes and falls still; the screaming, the pounding, go abruptly silent.

Sue doesn't move. There is one final gunshot, this one tearing straight through the lock, and she jumps so hard it hurts. From her side Sue sees the handle burst out of the door, then dangle crookedly like a broken crank on an old-time ice cream machine. She is slowly aware of the acrid smell of gunpowder seeping through the hole.

The entire planet holds its breath as nothing moves. Out there, Sue feels it waiting, knowing she's in here.

What's on the other side right now? What would I be looking at if that door weren't there? Dear God, what kind of gun-toting horror would I see staring back at me? Another fresh corpse, or the original one, the rotting scarecrow shape of the Engineer himself?

Slow, unhurried footsteps drag themselves down the hall, away from the room. Sue listens as they recede, growing softer, finally gone.

She touches the door.

It swings open about six inches, then stops, striking something. Sue looks down through the crack. The fluorescent lights in the hall seem marginally less

bright than those in the room, but she has no difficulty making out the sliver of blue fabric, a police
uniform stained darker, the white skin of a forearm
against the blood gleaming from the pale wood floor.

She pushes harder but the door doesn't budge. The
body of the cop remains tightly wedged against it.

With new resolve, Sue takes a step back and charges,
driving her shoulder forward and putting both legs
behind her, forcing the door open another six inches.
There's a wet, rough sound, like a damp sandbag
being dragged over gravel, as the body slides heavily
backward and then abruptly rolls onto its side, one
arm flopping over so the knuckles of its hands hit the
wall, the clack of the Fraternal Order of Police ring
striking against the plaster.

Sue recoils, ducking back into the room. The first
thought in her head is Jeff Tatum's corpse pouncing
on her outside of Babes. But the body on the floor
rolled only because of the way the door was pushing
it—although she can't see its face, which is turned to
the opposite wall, she can tell the corpse isn't moving
on its own.

Besides, she thinks, *the body hasn't gone through
the route. I mean, let's be logical here.*

"Logical," she mumbles. "Sure, yeah, you bet."

Still, she has to step over it to get out.

Bracing herself on the door frame, she raises her
right leg up over the dead cop and pivots her body
sideways so she can slide her hips through the opening. Her eyes go down to the blood on the floor.
Seems like more now than only a few seconds earlier.

It would be just like her to slip and fall in it, to land right on top of the corpse. Leaning farther, still clinging onto the frame behind her for support, Sue half-hops over the body and plants one foot and then the other safely on the floor.

She gives one backward glance at the body. It's the young cop with the thin blond mustache. Above the bridge of his nose, both eye sockets have been reduced to a bloody mash. A garish bouquet of arterial blood is splattered across the wall behind him, layered so thickly that it has begun to drip down toward the baseboard heating.

She runs down the hall, through the open doorway to the booking desk. Rounding the corner she sees the body of the booking sergeant slumped over the desk, arms shot out sideways at ridiculous angles, head wrenched down and to the left so that one of his blown-out eye sockets is partially visible from where she stands. The American flag behind him is covered in his blood and flecked intermittently with the gray mattress stuffing of what must be brain matter.

Farther to her right, beyond the desk, next to a pair of vending machines, another dead cop is sprawled on his stomach, a partially unwrapped Mars Bar clutched in his hand. Sue turns to the exit. There's yet another body between two potted ferns by the front door, lying next to an overturned table in a spray of old magazines and safety pamphlets. As she walks toward it Sue realizes that she's looking at Yates, both eyes blasted through the back of his skull, his beard transformed into a sodden mop of deep scarlet. His mouth is slightly open so she can see his tongue inside, blood on his teeth.

She strides toward the glass doors, toward the darkness beyond them, thinking that she's never been so relieved to see so little daylight in the sky, and that's when she hears the noise behind her. At first she doesn't recognize it because of the way it's being filtered, through a tinny speaker, like a pair of headphones cranked up to maximum volume. When she does figure it out, she realizes it's the sound of laughter and cheering, applause, and rhythmic music playing in the background.

Sue turns back toward the booking desk. The TV that was showing the old Clint Eastwood movie when she came in is still on. But the tape has been changed. Now the image on the screen—she can see it clearly from here—is of a naked woman onstage, running her hands over her stomach and breasts while the men in the crowd howl rabidly.

Sue frowns, looking closer, and just when she sees that the naked body onstage belongs to her, the taped footage breaks off.

There's an instant of snow.

Then a new image fills the screen.

Sue gazes at the TV monitor, unblinking. On-screen, the child strapped into the car seat is asleep, her head tucked to her chest. Sue sees at once that it's Veda.

The child doesn't appear hurt, just totally exhausted, sleeping deeply enough that the harsh glare of the video camera's light shining in her face doesn't even make her flinch. The camera holds its position and Sue notices that the time code streaming across the bottom of the screen reads 04:09 A.M., less than an hour earlier.

He taped that footage and he left it here.

She sees a hand enter the frame from the right, gently grasping Veda's head underneath her jaw and lifting it slightly upward to expose the soft white flesh of her throat.

For a moment Veda tenses, still asleep, trying to pull her head away, but then she just sighs and falls still again. Sue stares at the screen as another hand enters the picture, this time from the left side. It is holding a long, serrated knife.

"Oh God, no," Sue hears herself say, in a voice that doesn't sound like it belongs to her at all. "Don't you dare, you son of a bitch."

The hand holds the tip of the knife to Veda's neck, so close that it's impossible to discern whether the tip is touching her skin or not. All it has to do is push the blade upward, or let Veda's sleeping head drop down. But it holds the tableau, child and knife, for that breathless span of seconds.

"You promised," Sue says. "You *promised*."

Nothing on the screen moves. A moment later the image erupts in static. Sue is aware that she's leaning so far forward that she's in danger of falling over the desk. There's a sharp chirping sound on the counter next to her. She looks down.

It's her cell phone, the one that came with her new clothes. She grabs it, hits TALK. "You promised you wouldn't hurt her."

"You're letting your imagination run away with you, Susan," the voice says. "I always keep my promises. You know that by now, don't you?"

"I'll do whatever you want."

"I know you will. That's why I cleared the way for you." The voice chuckles, but there's no humor in it. "Even the Engineer needed a little guidance from time to time, Susan."

She looks at the bodies sprawled around the police station. *That's why I cleared the way for you.*

"You'll find your car in the impound lot behind the station. But you need to hurry. You've got a long way to go before sunrise."

She nods, grunting, and heads for the door. She's getting that vibe again, the feeling that the voice is waiting there on the other end even though it isn't saying anything. What's it waiting for, she wonders, a thank-you? Or is it waiting to see if she'll remember something she's forgotten?

She stops with one hand resting on the cold door handle, and thinks of the map.

Walking over to where Yates's body lies, she squats down and sticks her hand into his pants pocket but finds only his wallet and keys. She checks the other pockets. There's nothing but a disposable lighter and an almost-full pack of Marlboros, some wadded-up Kleenex, and loose change. Then something occurs to her, and she lifts the body up, rolling it onto its side. The floor beneath him is covered in blood.

The map is down there, pressed between his body and the floor, protected in the evidence baggie. In one smooth gesture Sue lifts it from the baggie and tucks it under one arm, puts her hands in the pockets of her unfamiliar wool coat, and heads back out the door.

5:05 A.M.

She climbs over the fence into the impound lot. It's brightly lit and full of wrecked vehicles, snow-capped ghosts of a dozen different traffic accidents, making the Expedition easy to find. It's the only one that hasn't sustained some kind of career-ending automotive trauma. She opens the driver's side door, hears the familiar chime. The keys are in the ignition, tagged with an orange piece of cardboard with her name and the date of impound written on it.

She needs to get out of here, but there's one other thing that she has to do first.

Leaving the door ajar, she walks around to the back of the Expedition and lifts the hatch, lowering her eyes swiftly for a look inside.

Marilyn's body is missing.

Is this a surprise? Not really. From what Yates told her, it sounded like they'd taken it out already. And under any other circumstances, on any other night, that fact alone would've been a sufficient explanation for why it was no longer here.

But Sue notices that the other body, the Engineer, *is*

still here—or moved *back* here, anyway—wrapped in his shroud of plastic garbage bags. The question arises: Why is he here while Marilyn is gone?

And the answer surges up from the animal part of her brain. The Engineer is her passenger, just as he's been her passenger for all these years, riding along in the back of her mind through whatever else was going on in her life. Because, she thinks, it is like Phillip says, the past is never done with us, not in any substantial way, and anybody who tells you otherwise hasn't taken a good look into their backseat lately.

But Marilyn, where is Marilyn?

As she climbs back into the driver's seat, from the corner of her eye Sue catches a shadow-flicker of motion off to the right, on the far side of the chain-link fence, twenty, maybe thirty yards away. The high-powered sodium lights end abruptly at the fence's perimeter, as if they don't have any interest in illuminating whatever lies beyond, but she can still make out a shadow of something trundling its way over the snowy hillside where it gives way to the access road. It's a human-size shadow, but it doesn't *move* like a human, or even an animal; it lumbers and flops its way along with the innate clumsiness of something stiff and inanimate being dragged across the snow, kicking up clouds of white powder as it advances blindly forward. Like an anchor dragging the ocean floor.

Sue's eyes chase the shadow over the snow between two pine trees, where it vanishes momentarily in a pool of darkness, then reappears on the other side,

right outside the police station. There's a vehicle waiting in the lot. She can see the beams of its headlights—
and then the shadow steps into their glare. From here
Sue can see the source of the shadow with undeniable
clarity.

It's Marilyn.

For a moment the woman who was her daughter's
nanny stands wavering in the headlights, hunched
stupidly forward, jaw slack, arms dangling at her sides.
She looks very old, very dead. Her hair is a greasy
ruin of kinks and angles, mashed unevenly against
one side of her skull, and dried blood covers her
cheeks and neck like a beard, staining the entire front
of her sweater.

Then with a slow shuffling of feet, Marilyn turns
herself until she's facing Sue. She's twitching her head
up and down with little sniffing gestures.

Is she smelling me? Sue wonders. Searching for my
scent?

She can't help but stare. Even from this distance
she's aware that the vacancies of Marilyn's eye sockets are not entirely empty anymore. There's a dark
gleam inside them, moving slightly, as her head jerks
up and down, as if some alien optic instrument were
incubating deep inside Marilyn's skull.

Her new eyes, Sue thinks. Her route eyes. They're
growing back.

Releasing Sue from that horrible myopic gleam,
Marilyn turns and slumps her way toward the em-
brace of the headlights. And though she's moving more
slowly now it's the same tree-stump stumble, lunging

forward and then catching herself, as if the tendons and ligaments aren't connected right anymore.

Then she stops again and turns herself back toward Sue.

What's she doing? It's like she's waiting for somebody to join her. But who else is here except for—

All at once a hand grabs her from behind.

5:11 A.M.

The fingers are cold, clamping over her mouth. A sudden tree of terror bursts from her spine upward through her chest, its branches spreading down her arms to her fingertips. The hand pulls her back against the headrest and flattens her lips against her teeth, compressing the scream that has no time to emerge. She writhes in the seat, trying to get free, but the grip is unyielding and she can't even turn her head. One of the fingers worms its way between her teeth and she tastes cold salt, dirt, and blood mingled together against her tongue. Simultaneously gagging and biting down, she shuts her eyes and feels tears springing up from them, her stomach clenching spasmodically.

Relaxing its grip slightly, the thing crawls up between the driver and passenger seats, and only then does Sue manage to twist her head enough to look over to see who it is. She spots the white T-shirt and bloodstained face. Then the smell hits her. A cloud of foulness clings to him so densely that it almost seems to pulsate from his flesh.

"Susan," Jeff Tatum says. "Remember me?"

She stares at him, her stomach roiling with nausea and shock. Like Marilyn's, his shot-out eyes are beginning to come back, and now Sue has a closer look at the results. Instead of empty sockets, there are now black, jellylike orbs quivering inside his skull, the way she imagines shark's eyes must when they're first beginning to take shape. What must the world look like through such eyes? she wonders bleakly.

"It's better this way, Susan. You'll see when you get here. You don't feel anything anymore. It's like the best drug you ever had."

He pulls away so she can respond. "What do you want?"

"I'm just a messenger, here to deliver a reminder."

"Which is what?"

His fingers go up to tease the tatters of flesh around his shimmering, embryonic new eyes. "To stay on the route, if you want to see your daughter again."

"When I saw you before, you told me not to go any farther."

The ruined face flushes with anger. Without the slightest warning he swings his right hand at her face, slamming her in the cheekbone, knocking her backward into the door. "Don't you *ever* fucking argue with me, you stupid bitch. I know what's best. I'll decide if your little Veda comes back to you dead or alive. Or have you forgotten that already?"

"No," Sue says levelly. "I haven't forgotten." The blow to the face has had a paradoxical effect of restoring some cruel kind of alertness; it occurs to her now that she might be able to use this moment to her advantage, if only in a minor way. "There's something else I haven't forgotten, either, Jeff."

"I'm not Jeff anymore. Jeff is gone."

It's an old poem. You have to remember it. It can help you.

And despite everything that's happening Sue finds herself mouthing the words. They come out as little more than a whisper—but they come out just the same.

"From Ocean Street in old White's Cove . . ."

"What's that? What did you say?" Jeff Tatum pauses, seeming to hesitate, his head cocked as if he's listening to some sound far off in the distance. A wave of uncertainty has come over his face, or what's left of it, reflected primarily in the looseness of his mouth.

"Across the virgin land he drove . . ."

Tatum flinches, averting his face, cringing from her like an old Universal Studios vampire from sunlight. "You ought to shut your mouth," he growls, but it doesn't sound like much of a demand. It's almost like a plea. She's vaguely aware of his voice becoming more boyish, less hateful, as he retreats.

Sue sits up, propping herself on her elbows. "To paint each town and hamlet red, with the dying and the dead—"

"*Stop it, I said!*" Tatum has moved away from her entirely, drawing his body toward the door, but he can't find the handle. "*You shut your mouth, you fucking stupid bitch!*"

"He walked through Wickham and Newbury."

She's speaking faster now, and louder too. "In Ashford or Stoneview he might tarry, to call a child to his knee, where he slew it—one, t—"

"Shut up, shut up, shut up!" At this point the thing has turned totally around to face the door and the voice is simply a shriek, pained and helpless. When he snaps his head back toward her again Sue sees something else emerging through the soulless sockets—an entirely new expression, the face of a young man awakening from a very realistic nightmare, perhaps one in which he has no eyes. He screams one final time, a protracted howl, and then falls silent. When he eventually raises his head to look at her, the only expression on his ruined face is puzzlement.

"Ms. Young?" Jeff's voice is quiet, gentle. "Are you there?"

"Jeff."

"What happened to me? Was there an accident? I don't remember anything. We were talking, and then—"

"It's all right."

"No, it isn't. I can tell." He turns his head to the right and left as if he's hoping to see something through his hideous new eyes. "What happened to my eyes? Is it bad?"

"Can you see anything?"

"Yes, I can see but . . . everything's red and shiny, like it's wet." He pauses. "Everything's covered in blood."

Sue nods. "There was an accident."

"Listen, Ms. Young, you need to listen to me. Turn around. You can't go any farther down this route."

"Jeff, I need to ask you about Isaac Hamilton and the Engineer. What's he trying to do here?"

"Hamilton," Jeff says.

"Yes, Jeff—Isaac Hamilton. What's he doing?"

"His victims. The route brings them back. Then Hamilton takes them. Takes *us*." From deep in his chest he produces a harsh, humorless cackle, and she's losing him now, she can feel it. "Windows to the soul. That's what he says."

"The Engineer?"

Jeff's mouth opens, makes a weak gasping sound. The sound becomes: ". . . Hamilton."

"Wait," Sue says, "so was Isaac Hamilton controlling the Engineer?"

"You . . . you can't . . ." His voice falters, stranded between words, and Sue hears an edge creeping back into it. Beneath the crusted blood Jeff Tatum's mouth pinches tight, the muscles left in his jaw tensing, as if he's struggling with something, another voice that only he can hear.

"*No*. Shut up. I don't *want* to."

"Jeff?"

"I don't . . . No, you're lying, you're lying, *you're lying to me*—" And all at once his hands fly up, plunging his fingers into his own black eyes, and his voice explodes with a scream. "*NO!*" The scream drags out, dissipating and becoming a wild, hysterical laugh.

Sue doesn't wait for the transformation. Twisting around sideways in her seat she plants both feet on Tatum's bloody chest and propels him backward into his door, and while he's jammed against it, still in the throes of whatever inner turmoil is ripping him apart, she lunges forward and pulls on the handle. The door swings wide and he tumbles backward out of the Expedition. Sue yanks the door shut, slams down the lock.

The poem is like a charm. It beats him back.

In front of the Expedition she sees Jeff flash through her headlights, but he's not coming for her. He's headed toward the fence. In seconds he's over it, scurrying past the police station and into the headlights of the van waiting beyond.

Across the hollow winter night Sue hears a metal door slide open, then shut again a moment later. An engine revs, grows louder, and then pulls away. She thinks of Marilyn. Is she in there too, with Jeff and Veda?

Sue looks into the back of the Expedition at her own passenger, waiting to see how the rest of the night will play itself out. It's just her and the Engineer, straight to the end of the line. They don't have much time left.

"All right, you sadistic piece of shit," Sue says. "Let's hit the road."

5:21 A.M.

Wickham, according to the map, lies about thirty miles northeast, the dogleg road bending upward as it makes its way toward East Newbury and ultimately to White's Cove. At this point Sue takes nothing on faith except the too-dumb-to-die possibility that she might actually get her daughter back if she completes this lunatic errand on time. Beyond that, any and all logic and preconceived ideas have left the building. She blocks out everything but the road, the endless road, the yellow lines pulsing along through her windshield. It's hypnotic.

Without warning Sue experiences a deep sense of fatigue, like a lead apron settling over her head and shoulders. She's been awake for almost twenty-four hours; her body has chosen this moment to make her aware of this fact. When her alarm went off yesterday morning at six A.M., no amount of drugs and horror movies could have suggested what lay ahead of her before she'd be able to sleep again. Suddenly her eyelids feel like they're swelling to cover her eyes; her head tilts forward, then snaps back, as if from a vicious blow.

Reaching under her seat she finds a half bottle of Poland Spring water, ice cold. She unscrews the cap and sucks it down in great, greedy gulps until her throat throbs and starts to go numb. Her skull pounds but at least she no longer feels like she's about to pass out.

She thinks about Tatum, the urgency with which the human side of him seemed to want to impart some further information to her. What was it? She very much doubts that she'll get another chance to find out.

Her eyes flick randomly from the windshield across the dashboard.

Then she remembers the cassette.

Jeff Tatum stuck it in the tape deck right before her cell phone rang and the shooting started. It's no wonder she forgot about it. It's been tucked invisibly inside the console all this time. She switches the player back on, the tape rolling, and hears the DJ's voice start up again:

". . . playing all your requests straight on through this miserably hot August night. I don't know about you folks, but I can't sleep when the nights get sticky like this. So for all you insomniacs out there, crank up the AC, crack open another cold one, and call me up with the songs you want to hear. I'll do my best to get us through the night, okay? Let's go to the phones. Hello, who's this?"

"This is Jeff from Gray Haven." It's Tatum's voice,

no question, accompanied by a tooth-aching screech of feedback. "I've got a—"

"Hey, Jeff, can you do me a favor and turn your radio down, pal? We're picking up a lot of squeal back here."

"Huh? Oh, sorry."

"No problem, Jeff. What can I play for you on this hot summer's eve, buddy?"

"I was wondering if you could play 'Daniel,' by Elton John."

"Elton John?" DJ Damien laughs. "Whoa, Jeff, I think you got the wrong station, my friend. We're strictly modern rock here."

"It's for my little brother," Tatum's voice says. "He died three years ago. His name was Daniel."

The DJ pauses. "I'm sorry to hear that, Jeff."

"The Engineer killed him."

Now the pause is longer. Sue can sense the DJ trying to formulate some kind of diplomatic reply. "Excuse me, Jeff. Did you say the Engineer killed your brother?"

"That's right."

"Three years ago?"

"To the day."

"Jeff, are you aware that the Engineer hasn't killed anybody since 1983?"

"That's not true," Jeff Tatum's voice says patiently. "He *disappeared* in August of 1983—in fact the last killing he was connected with happened right in my town on August 22 of that year—but his body was never found. And since then he's resurfaced more than once. The police just haven't put two and two together."

"Is that a fact?" DJ Damien sounds dubious, to say the least. "So you're actually telling us that the Engineer is connected with killings but the police in the area somehow haven't noticed?"

"I tried going to the cops," Jeff's voice says. "They told me I was crazy."

"Imagine," DJ Damien says.

"I'm serious." If Jeff's aware he's being made fun of, he doesn't show it. "It was him."

"What makes you so sure?"

"He always shoots out the eyes."

"Have you ever heard the term *copycat,* Jeff?"

"This was no copycat. No coincidence, either. He left the body where the police would find it. Then, after the funeral, he dug the body up again. It disappeared. Just like the kids in 1983."

"You're kidding, aren't you, Jeff?" DJ Damien asks. "Hey, Jeff?" There's a long pause, too long, before Damien seems to realize he's talking to a dead line. "All right, I guess we've heard the end of that; what do the rest of you think? Come on, folks, it's two A.M., our sponsors have all gone to bed, it's dead silent out there, what else is there to talk about besides mass murder?" Sue can hear him sigh. "Meanwhile, for Jeff in Gray Haven, here's the song I wouldn't normally play under any circumstances."

And Sue hears "Daniel" start playing. She waits, watching the broken yellow line jumping on the other side of her windshield, snow flickering through it, and when the song ends, Damien comes back on.

"Well, children, like it or not, it seems tonight's topic has become the Engineer. Honest to God, people, I never would've dreamt there were so many of you out there with an opinion on this. Hello, you're live on the X midnight shift, who's this?"

"This is Vicky. I'm working third-shift out in Woburn."

"Vicky, what do you think about what our pal Jeff said about the Engineer?"

"I think the guy's onto something."

"So you think the Engineer's still out there?"

"Absolutely. I think I dated him."

Damien laughs. "All right, thanks a lot." He goes to the next call. "Hey, the X, who's this?"

"This is Randall."

"Where you calling from, Randall?"

"Dorchester."

"Randall, what's your take on the Engineer, dead or alive?"

"It's irrelevant."

Damien makes a yawning sound. "Fascinating answer, Randall. Thanks for weighing in."

"I'm totally serious. To understand the Engineer you have to know about Isaac Hamilton. That's the real story."

"Never heard of him."

"That's because no one pays attention to the tabloids," Randall says. "Hamilton's the guy whose statue is up in all seven towns that the Engineer went through, from White's Cove right to Gray Haven. Whoever the Engineer was, you can't tell me he wasn't influenced by Hamilton."

"All I said was, I never heard of the guy. Suppose you enlighten us."

"Well . . ." Randall holds back a second, considering his reply. "Let's just say that what Isaac Hamilton did back in the late eighteenth century makes the Engineer look like a Boy Scout by comparison. Depending on what account you read, he put away something like twenty, twenty-five kids in his day."

"How intriguing," DJ Damien says, though Sue doesn't think he sounds intrigued. He sounds like he wishes he never started this conversation. "Okay, I'm going to take a couple more calls on this, children, and then we're going to move on to a more wholesome topic like, oh, I don't know, famous celebrity suicides. Hello, you're on the air, who's this?"

"This is Terry from Chelmsford."

"Terry, I hope you've got something down to earth to say on this topic that can help put the rest of these paranoid freaks at ease."

Terry gives a high-pitched little giggle, the giggle of a man, Sue thinks, wired to the eyeballs on an all-night binge of coffee, cigarettes, and nothing to do. "As a matter of fact, I read a history book about Isaac Hamilton," he says. "As far as the connection between the Engineer and Hamilton goes, I don't see how you can ignore it."

"Is that so. I guess the police managed to overlook all this when they were hunting the Engineer?"

"No, they know about it, they just don't have the imagination to put it in context."

"Uh-huh."

"I'm serious. This book talked about how Hamilton was, like, this sea captain in the days of whaling and how he ended up in Haiti way back in the late 1700s."

"Gripping stuff, Terry, but—"

"It said when he came back to Boston he was already going crazy from a wicked case of syphilis, but the voodoo priests taught him the so-called secrets of everlasting life."

"I'm sorry, did you say *voodoo priests,* Terry?"

"It's pretty obvious to anybody who does a little reading that wherever the Engineer is right now, Isaac Hamilton is with him, firing up the old barbecue grill. So if you live between White's Cove and Gray Haven, watch your back!"

"Thanks a bunch, Terry. What are you people on tonight, anyway? Okay, one more call. Who is this?"

There's a long pause on the other end.

"Hello, caller? You there?"

"Hello?"

"While we're young, caller. Let's start with your name."

"You want to know my name?" The caller's voice is formal, anxious. Sue recognizes it instantly. The realization sucks the breath from her lungs in one unpleasant tug, leaves her with nothing but a dry ache where her heart should be.

She stops the tape, hits REWIND, and plays it back to make sure, but that's not really necessary.

"You want to know my name?"

She knows it immediately. She would've recognized it from a single syllable, perhaps not even that.

The caller is Phillip.

"That's right, what's your name?" the DJ asks patiently.

Phillip clears his throat. "I'd rather not give it, if that's all right with you."

"Suit yourself, mystery man. Can you tell us where you're calling from on this disgustingly hot August night, or is that classified top secret too?"

"Not that it matters, but I'm listening to a webcast of your show. I'm in California."

"Fantastic. Just keep it short, huh?"

"I'm responding to the callers who seem to believe that the child-killer known as the Engineer might still be alive somewhere, possibly due to supernatural reasons, simply because he was never apprehended and his body was never found."

"Okay . . ."

"Trust me, this is not the case. I was born and raised in Gray Haven, and I can assure you beyond the slightest shadow of a doubt that the Engineer is dead. He died—a long time ago."

"You sound pretty sure of yourself there," Damien says. "What, do you have proof or something?"

Sue can't believe she's hearing this. She resists the temptation to stop the tape again and rewind, to try listening from the beginning, because there's no point. There's no way the man talking on this call-in show from six months earlier is not her husband.

"Like I said," Phillip says, "I grew up in Gray Haven. I was there when everything happened. For those who didn't live through it, it's almost impossible to convey the atmosphere of pure dread that existed during that summer. Thirteen children murdered, including one in our own town; police had zero leads, no identification, no physical description of the killer beyond the fact that he wore overalls and looked like a locomotive engineer."

"Yeah, we all know the history, chief."

Phillip just ignores him. "The mood those days was almost borderline hysteria. Curfews were established and parents refused to let their children out of the yard, even in broad daylight. Those of us who were old enough to follow what was happening speculated all the time about who might be next."

"Uh-huh."

"Then on August 21 my friend and I were out on one of the back roads, hanging out at this old playground on the edge of town—a stupid idea considering everything that was going on. Anyway, we saw a car idling alongside the fence. It looked like a Plymouth, and it was burnt orange. We noticed that the man inside was wearing overalls and—"

"Whoa, whoa, whoa," Damien cuts in, "hold on here. Are you actually going to tell me that you and this buddy of yours saw the Engineer in person?"

"That's right."

"Unbelievable. So what did you do?"

"We discussed for several minutes what should be done, whether we should alert the police about the man. I won't go into the specifics of what happened next, except that it wasn't long before we no longer had a choice."

"What do you mean—you no longer had a choice?"

There's a long silence hissing from the tape, long enough for Sue to think, *Don't say it, Phillip. Don't you dare say what I think you're about to.*

"That afternoon," Phillip says, "my friend and I killed the Engineer."

"Excuse me?" Damien says. "You did *what*?"

"It was horrible and we never spoke of it to anyone, including the police. But the murders stopped after that, so we know it was him."

"Hold on, go back—"

"First we got rid of the car. I was only eleven but I got up behind the wheel and drove it out to an empty field by the edge of a forest. We took everything out of the car and dumped it. Then we went back and buried the body where we knew it would never be found." He stops as if to gather his thoughts and pull himself together. "To those who delight in such things I say only that the Engineer isn't some supernatural ghoul or bogeyman under the bed. He was a sick man who liked to kill children, and he is now very, very dead."

"Stop, hang on a damn second," Damien says. "You honestly expect us to believe that you and your pal killed the Engineer and stashed the body and that's why the killings stopped? *That's* your story?" He waits. "Hello, caller? Are you there . . . ?"

But Phillip is gone. Sue hears DJ Damien let out a long sigh, audibly shaken. "Well, children, I think I can safely say that this has been one of the strangest midnight shifts in recent memory. I'm going to throw on some tunes and pour myself a *big* cup of coffee. Not to belabor the obvious, here's Rob Zombie with 'Living Dead Girl.' And for all of you insomniac freaks and geeks out there, the topic of the Engineer is officially closed."

Sue hears grinding guitar cut in and, within a few seconds, the recording ends. She fast-forwards briefly but there's nothing more on the tape.

"Phillip," she says. "Why did you have to tell them? What were you *thinking*?"

Of course she knows the answer already. Phillip made his anonymous confession to DJ Damien and the insomniac listeners for the same reason he woke up bathed in sweat night after night, screaming or close to it. Because he needed to. Because the past is never done with us, not in any substantial way.

She can see it now. To her post-exhausted mind, it all clicks with a kind of chilling certainty, a puzzle whose pieces can't possibly fit together in any other way. She knows that Phillip never got past what happened that afternoon between them and the Engineer. For him, calling in to this show would be a combination of relief and self-flagellation, touching on old scars that had never quite healed. She imagines him on the other side of the continent, hunkered over his phone, drinking black coffee and poring over the old photos and scanned news items from the past, reliving the terror that they both felt so acutely that summer.

For as long as possible he must have tried to cope with his fears that he was being followed, sublimating them into nightmares. And when he couldn't stand it anymore he'd done the one thing he thought he must do—he'd left Sue and their baby girl with the simplest excuse imaginable, abandonment, gave up everything and tried to disappear, for their own protection. He went to California. Severed every tie save the most essential ones. Communicated with her only by phone and e-mail.

Until that night back in August when he called in to the radio show. It wasn't long after that that Sue stopped hearing from him completely.

Almost without realizing it, she passes the sign on the right:

WICKHAM—ESTABLISHED 1802

If not for the sign, she would have thought she took a wrong turn. Of all the stops along the route, Wickham is the most developed yet. It's almost quaint. Down the main thoroughfare she can see a toy store, a real estate office, clothing boutiques, and a pizza parlor, all with hand-painted wooden signs hanging down that remind her of the storefronts of Concord Center. On the right is an ice cream place, and next to it a bookshop called Bound to Please.

It's still dark, of course, and she doesn't see any residents, but there's a smattering of lights on in the windows of Main Street. Sue tries to think. Are the towns along the route also coming to life as she enters them?

Up ahead she can see a snow-dusted triangle of ground, slightly raised, with the main road bending around it. In the center, bracketed by park benches, is a pedestal with a figure on top of it. Isaac Hamilton, who else could it be? And from here she can see clearly that the figure has no arms or legs, just a slender body with head, held up at the same proud tilt. At least the angle of the head *used* to look proud to her; now it looks defiant. As she lowers her foot on the brake, the Expedition's tires encounter an unexpected patch of black ice and the vehicle swerves a little. Sue instinctively steers in the direction of the skid, correcting it without thinking—ambulance driver reflexes coming into play again.

Then, halfway through Wickham, as she passes the statue, it starts snowing again, heavily. She sits forward, switches on her wipers, visibility compromised. The flakes are thick and seem to strike her windshield with real weight. It's becoming distinctly more difficult to see.

Up ahead, at the next intersection, the gray van is pulling out of a side street, emerging from a snowfall so thick that it actually seems to materialize out of the air. It turns right, and now it's driving in front of her, fifty feet up the road, heading out of town. The van is moving slower than she is and she taps the brake slightly to maintain her distance. At the same time the snow falls even harder, thicker. The wipers are at their fastest setting and they still can't keep up. Sue slows down even more, hovering between twenty-five and thirty. The van's taillights fade in the distance, and then they are gone. She feels pressure in her skull, building in her sinuses. It's her headache coming back. Her foot goes down on the gas. She's going thirty-five, forty.

Sue's still picking up speed when the snow suddenly stops coming down again, the road clear in front of her. With complete clarity she sees the van is right there, less than twenty feet away.

It's directly in her path.

And it's not moving.

"Shit!" She grabs the wheel with both hands and smashes down on the brake. The Expedition goes into a skid, the back end swerving, coming around faster than she can control it, and Sue realizes there's no choice—she's going to hit the van, and she's going to hit it hard. Everything slows down, the details of the moment laser-clear in her mind, and there's a loud, complicated crash as the rear of the Expedition smacks violently into the van. The impact hurls her hard against the seat belt, which catches her between her breasts, the Expedition's airbag deploying with a pop that she feels more than hears, the synthetic smell of fresh plastic whacking her in the face and driving her head back against the seat. Then it's deflating, letting her sag forward, as she looks out her windshield at nothing. The engine has stalled. It's dead quiet.

Sliding out of her seat, she jumps down and walks around the back of the Expedition. From here she can see that the rear door of the van has been knocked open and hangs crookedly from its hinges. There's a faint light on inside. Sue takes two steps, hearing her feet scrape the snow off the road as she advances toward the van, then cranes her neck for a closer look.

All the seats have been removed, creating a featureless cave. Sprawled on the floor, not moving, are two corpses that by now she recognizes immediately—her nanny, Marilyn, and Jeff Tatum. Marilyn is on her side, her legs flopped at an angle, one arm across her face. Jeff Tatum is facedown.

There's nothing else back here.

Keeping her distance, Sue walks sideways around the van. She sees a child's car seat on the front passenger side.

Veda's car seat.

It's empty.

The driver's seat is empty as well.

Sue slowly opens the passenger door, leaning in, placing one hand on the padded car seat, fingertips brushing over the stale cracker crumbs and dried raisins that have found their way into its creases over the months. The fabric upholstery is still warm. Pressing her nose against the seat's headrest, Sue smells

Veda's hair, where the back of her skull probably lay just a few seconds earlier.

Veda, what did they do with you? Where are you now?

Behind her in the darkness, she hears the trill of the cell phone in the Expedition. She starts walking toward it and thinks she sees something moving in the back of the vehicle, the shape in the garbage bags sitting upright against the rear window.

Watching her.

S ue blinks, squinting. It's too dark to tell whether she's imagining him there or not. Up front the phone is still ringing. That's definitely real. She opens the driver's side door, takes the phone, and steps away. Her headache is gone again, drowned in adrenaline.

Sue hits TALK.

"Where's my daughter?"

"Oh, that's right," the voice on the other end says. "You thought she was in the van, didn't you? Well, it's a good thing she wasn't, Susan. You could've really hurt her when you crashed into it." He pauses. "But if I were you, I wouldn't worry about where she is now, just where you're going to be in another ninety minutes, when her life is on the line."

"White's Cove. I'll be there."

"That's good," the voice says. "Meanwhile it looks like your passenger is showing some life of his own."

She glances into the back of the Expedition. The shape against the glass is no longer there. He must've lain down again or lost his strength. Maybe he wasn't sitting up at all. Walking to the driver's side, the phone clasped to her ear, Sue looks in but doesn't see the thing in the garbage bags poking its head up. The Expedition is silent inside. She climbs behind the wheel, starts the engine. "You want me to—"

"Get back on the road," the voice on the other end says. "Get moving."

Sue puts the Expedition in gear. She drives the rest of the way out of town. The yellow lines leap through her headlights, behind the snow, a peculiar feeling of dislocation filtering through her mind. Something is happening here. She's going forward, but she's also traveling backward. Backward in time, more than twenty years, to the day that she and Phillip saw the man at the park. This is not a voluntary remembrance. It's like the memory is being leached from her pores.

Looking through the windshield of the Expedition, Sue can already make out the worn-out assortment of leftover playground equipment through eleven-year-old eyes, wilting in the muggy heat of that lost August afternoon. She and Phillip were sitting on the cracked plastic swings, idly kicking their legs at the small patches of muddy earth underneath them, the last remnants of a weak rain two days earlier. Twenty yards away, two younger children, scrubby-looking toddlers in dirty shirts and skinned knees, giggled and shrieked as they ran up and down through the low weeds while their mothers, mobile-home women in Spandex pants, watched anxiously, smoking cigarettes.

They were the only other kids here. Most people had stopped letting their children venture beyond the center of town that summer. Instead they went to the movies or the mall or played at Sheckard Park in the middle of town, or their parents packed them off to band camp or chauffeured them to the gated community pool two towns over. Sue's mother didn't know that she and Phillip had ridden their bikes out here today—she thought they were at the East Town Mall catching a matinee—and Phillip's parents . . . well, Phillip's parents never really seemed to question where Phillip was. When in doubt, they assumed that he was at the public library, studying. And more often than not, they were right.

But today, he and Sue had come out here to sit on the swings, kick their feet up and catch a too-infrequent breeze lifting from the empty field down the road, bringing the smell of industrial solvents from the mill in town. Phillip had bought them both Cokes from the 7-Eleven on the bike ride out, the wet plastic bottles covered with dirt and wood chips. Sue wasn't sure why they'd come here, except that they liked it—the conversations they had here seemed different from any conversation she ever had with anybody else, ever. Sure, she and Phillip would talk about school and TV, and how screwed up their parents were. But they also talked a lot about the future— Phillip had already decided he was going to be some kind of millionaire, Sue said she wanted to be an Alaskan bush pilot or possibly a doctor. Sometimes they didn't talk about anything at all, just sat in comfortable silence.

It was during one of those silences, disturbed only

by the soft creak of the swings, when Phillip had glanced up and said, almost conversationally, "Hey. Do you recognize that car?"

Sue looked past the dirty playground equipment over to the flattened patch of dirt that served as a parking lot. She saw two run-down cars that the trailer-park moms had arrived in, a rusted-out Chevy and a Ford station wagon with fake wood paneling, parked right in front of the gate. Across the lot, in the shadow of a giant elm tree, sat a long, boxy sedan, a Plymouth or something, she wasn't sure. It was burnt orange with a black roof. From where she and Phillip sat now, there was just enough of a glare on the windshield that she couldn't tell whether or not there was someone behind the wheel.

"It's been there for a while," Phillip said. "It pulled up right after we got here. Did you notice?"

Sue shook her head, still swinging back and forth, dragging the toes of her Chuck Taylors in the cracked and drying mud. She *hadn't* noticed, which was strange—her mother was always telling her what an observant girl she was. But the Plymouth had arrived so silently that it must have completely escaped her attention. Like it materialized out of nowhere, she thought, and shivered.

"What if it's him?" Phillip asked abruptly.

She glanced at him. "Cut it out."

"I'm serious. You know he's out there somewhere. It could be him."

"Oh, please," Sue said, in the drabbest voice she could muster. They almost never talked about the

Engineer. Not because it scared them, but quite the opposite—it was old news, almost boring to them. All summer the Engineer was all that everybody in town talked about, certainly their parents and teachers and neighbors never gave the topic a rest.

He jumped off his swing. "I'm going over there to check it out."

"Oh, right." She was used to this from him. "What are you going to do, tap on the glass and ask him, Excuse me, do you mind if I check your trunk for human heads?"

"He always goes for the eyes," Phillip said, not looking back at her. "He shoots them out. He doesn't keep souvenirs."

"That's disgusting."

"It's true and you know it. It's in all the papers. And he only gets kids twelve and under."

Sue stopped swinging. Phillip was still walking briskly away from her, headed through the high grass toward the makeshift parking lot, and that was when she realized that he was serious. He was really going. The clarity of his intention startled her so much that the first word out of her mouth—"Wait!"—came out garbled and almost inaudible. Jumping off the swing, she cleared her throat and hurried to catch up.

"Phillip, what do you think you're doing?"

"Just what I said. I'm going to check it out."

"You can't do that."

He cocked an eyebrow at her. "Why not?"

She sighed. It was his favorite question, and half the time she couldn't answer it. She decided to discard whatever remained of her sarcastic detachment and address the issue head-on. "Okay, what if it is the guy?"

"What's he going to do, jump out of the car and grab me?" Phillip asked, not slowing his pace. "In broad daylight?"

"We're pretty far from town."

"Come on," he said, and if he was less sure of himself, he didn't let on.

"So what are you going to do?"

"I'm going to walk by, like I'm headed to the field, and as I pass him, just kind of take a look inside, see what he looks like. Maybe he's wearing the bib overalls with the blue stripes on them like that kid back in Wickham said."

"Yeah, I'm sure that's exactly what he's wearing," Sue said, not exactly sure why she was so reluctant to let Phillip get close to the Plymouth, only that the feeling of apprehension was building in her chest and abdomen, the way her head felt when she dove all the way to the bottom of the deep end of a pool. "Come on, let's just go—okay?"

For the first time he stopped and stared back at her. His dark eyes were serious, as grown-up as she'd ever seen them, and all at once she knew exactly what he was going to look like as a grown man—it might've even been the first time that she realized she loved him, a little.

"What if it happens tonight?" he asked. "And in the morning everybody's talking about some kid that got killed by the Engineer, and we both know we could've done something about it but we didn't. Do you want that on your conscience?"

She took a breath, considered any number of possible replies: *That's not going to happen* or *My conscience has nothing to do with this* or simply the ever-popular *Oh please,* but in the end she didn't say anything. They were a dozen steps from the edge of the bare, tire-packed earth, putting them twenty or thirty good strides from the orange Plymouth, and it was clear now that she wasn't going to stop him.

She glanced back over her shoulder to where the toddlers and their mothers had been playing, but the dingy little playground was empty. The blue Chevy and the rusty Ford were gone, must have left while she and Phillip were talking. The only car left in the lot was the Plymouth.

Sue nodded. "If we see anything that looks funny, we run straight to the police. I mean it, Phillip."

"No duh, genius," he smirked. "I'm not Magnum, PI."

"Yeah, you're more like Higgins." The banter, however lame, made her feel a little better, and the next thought was even more comforting. *Of course it's not going to be the Engineer in there. Phillip could go up to the guy, climb in the backseat and ask him what he thought about the Red Sox's chances for the playoffs,* it wouldn't matter because there's no way the man that killed a dozen kids is sitting right there, twenty feet away from us.

No, of course not. It wasn't the Engineer, it was just some worker bee from the paper mill, some lunch-box-toting working stiff like her own father who came down here to eat his onion sandwich and maybe sneak a warm Bud before going back to the factory floor. And when they got up to the orange Plymouth, Phillip would see that for himself.

Sue was still reassuring herself with these thoughts when the driver's side door opened and the man in blue-striped bib overalls looked out at them, and smiled.

6:38 A.M.

Sue sits up fast, eyes wide open, panic dousing her like an ice-cold jet of water, shooting down both arms and fusing her spinal column into a steel rod. The road is jumping at her crookedly—so crookedly that it's not the road at all, it's a thick row of trees plowing in her headlights, and she jerks the wheel hard around, the Expedition's back tires skidding but finding something to pull against under the ice. And she's back on course, breathing fast, trying not to have a heart attack.

She checks the dashboard clock. How long has she been out?

A few seconds, she thinks. Certainly no longer. It wasn't like she was dozing, though. It was more like being *gone*, transported, spirited away back to that summer day in '83. She can practically smell the metallic rust from the swing's chains on her palms and the high, acrid stench of the mill hanging in the air, the swamp below the bridge not far away. And despite the fact that it's got to be at least ten below outside with the wind chill, and the Expedition's broken side window is letting in all kinds of cold air, Sue realizes that underneath these strange, ill-fitting clothes she's filmed from scalp to ankles in a clinging layer of sweat. Not perspiration—kids didn't perspire, not even girls. They sweated.

The phone rings. She grabs it.

"Wake up, Susan."

"I'm awake," she croaks.

"You were drifting a little there," the voice chides. "Can't have that. Not with Veda relying on you to keep her alive."

"Why can't you tell me where she is?" Sue blurts, just defenseless enough from her vision of August 1983 that the question comes out sounding helpless. It sounds, actually, like a child's question, in a child's voice. "I just want to know she's all right."

"She's all right, Susan. As long as you stay on the road and don't crash into any trees, she'll be just dandy."

"I don't believe you."

"Always keep my promises, Susan," the voice says. "The only thing that matters is you. Getting you and your cargo where you need to be. At the other end of this route."

"Why is that so important to you?"

"Why?" She anticipates scorn, maybe even laughter, but his earnestness sounds genuine. "You ought to know that by now. I've been in this business for a long, long time. I'm an old hand at it, nearly as old as the country itself. Haven't you realized that yet?"

Sue lowers her hand from her mouth, looking for

the first time at the cell phone she's been holding against her face. It's a small, sleek device, chrome-colored, made by the good people at AT&T Wireless. She peers at the three little holes where the voice has come out, imagines being able to somehow shimmy through those invisible cell frequencies to wherever the voice is crouched, with her daughter at its side and a blade to Veda's throat.

"Isaac Hamilton," she says. "That's you, isn't it?"

"Ah. Now we're getting somewhere."

"It's been you the whole time."

"The whole time," the voice echoes, and there's something almost soothing about the ease with which his voice dovetails with hers. "Oh Susan, if only you knew how close you were. You know, I actually think you might make it."

Up ahead the road dips and rises and she can see the white sign for EAST NEWBURY—ESTABLISHED 1802, and she's not sure whether he's talking about making it through the route or—something else. Something deeper, reaching upward from the depths of her mind and heart simultaneously, two hands groping for a light switch in the dark. She knows the switch is there and when she hits it everything will leap into absolute clarity, despite the fact that she hasn't found it yet. But now, unexpectedly, irrationally, the urge to find out the truth overwhelms her, rivaling—even momentarily eclipsing—the urge to save her daughter's life.

"These towns on the route, they were all founded the same year, 1802," she says, passing the sign as she sees the first houses of town. "The year that . . ." Her mind flashes back to what one of the callers from the radio show said: *the late eighteenth century.* "The year they finally stopped you."

"The year they *killed* me, Susan."

"Who?"

"The idiots, the Puritans, the vultures, that pious, mindless, shrieking mob," he says. "They interrupted my work because they couldn't appreciate the holiness, the sanctity of what I was doing. And in the end they killed me for it. But I showed them, Susan, didn't I? Didn't I just?"

Sue waits, not saying anything. Outside her windows the haphazardly spliced landscape of East Newbury is tripping past in a series of flat, stacked row houses and narrow streets with cars piled in snow, but she couldn't be less aware of it. She can't even be slowed down. Her mind is warping ahead, switched on and powered up, and she's making connections more quickly than she's even consciously aware of. "The parents of the children," she says. "The children that you murdered."

"I deal in souls, Susan, always have. I harvest them the way a farmer harvests fruit, at the peak of its ripeness. The ripeness of childhood. I tried to explain that to them but the Philistines didn't understand my work. They *never* understood. It was like reciting sonnets to an orangutan or playing Bach cantatas for a chunk of granite. That's why I had to keep coming back, to make them understand the holiness of it."

"Coming back," she says.

"Three times the jackals came after me. The first

time they caught me was in the winter of 1793, four years after the holy men from Haiti had begun the painful process of awakening me to my mission on earth."

"Wait," Sue says, "go back," and she's zooming again to the tape of the call-in show, the mention of the voodoo priests. "What happened in Haiti?"

"In 1789 I was seventeen years old, and I signed on as a cook's apprentice on a whaler out of New Bedford. I was looking for adventure and I found it, certainly, but not the kind that I'd imagined. The cook turned out to be a leering pederast, a flabby, sadistic wolf with a taste for boys." The voice reels all this off with a keening, singsong inflection, as if the words themselves were some traditional ballad that he's been rehearsing over and over throughout the centuries. "On the first week of the voyage the perverted son of a bitch locked me in the galley with three of the mates, having charged each one a good bit of coin for the privilege, and they did what men do to the youngest boy on the vessel. I contracted a case of raging syphilis from one or perhaps all of them, I don't know—in any case I became very sick and by the sixth week of the voyage the crew abandoned me at a port in Haiti. I wandered inland and met the natives who lived there. They took pity on me."

"What did they do?"

"They made me well again."

"What did they do?" Sue repeats.

This time he ignores the question. "It wasn't long before I was able to arrange passage on another ship returning to my homeland. Upon finally arriving back I was a bit confused. But clarity returned to me in time, and I began to see my place in the greater warp and weft of creation."

"A harvester of souls," Sue hears herself say emptily.

"Oh yes," the voice replies. "And those were heady days, Susan, I wish you could've seen me then. My very first kill was a man named Gideon Winter, a perfect stranger. Killing him was merely a test, a means by which I could measure my own abilities and fortitude. After that I began to visit the families of the men who'd abandoned me. Many of my fellow sailors had gone back out to sea in the meantime, leaving their wives at home with many, many children—oh, I fattened myself upon their souls for months!"

"Their souls . . ." Sue begins. She can hear her own voice quavering uncontrollably. "They make you stronger?"

"Not just stronger, Susan. I absorb every soul that passes through me. I learn things from them. Languages, technologies—"

"Wait a minute," she says. "So this is how you found me? By murdering tech geeks?"

But again Hamilton ignores her, all but turning his back on the question. "After those first families in the Boston area, I ventured west through the young country, taking from it as I pleased, until one winter evening when a merchant found me in his barn, where I'd taken the eyes of his three young sons. I had them laid out in the most tantalizing tableau—really, you ought to have seen them, Susan. In any case, the merchant gathered a group from town and they nailed the door shut and set fire to the barn, burned it to the ground with me inside."

"What happened?" Sue asks.

Well, I died, Susan, obviously."

She waits.

"But my work would not let me rest. And so I came back five years later, on the twenty-second of December, to pick up where I left off. The restorative properties of my body had regenerated the dead, blackened skin that the fire had enshrouded me in, and I was ready to get back to business."

"Business," she says.

"Again, children, that ripest of fruit. This time I gathered seventeen more souls before the brutes tracked me down in a Boston wharf. A veritable army of longshoremen stabbed me dozens of times with gaffs and spears and various whaling implements until every drop of blood had drained from my body. They strung my mangled corpse from a ship's mast until the gulls plucked out my eyes and the flesh puckered and peeled from my bones. When they finally cut me down, they cast me into the sea with my legs weighted down in anchor chains, and I sank swiftly to the bottom. Food for the fishes, alas."

"And you came back again," Sue says.

The voice offers a quick grunt of assent. "What you must understand about me, Susan—what has eluded your fellow lower life-forms over the past two centuries—is that while I was in Haiti, I not only suffered from syphilis, *I died from it*. The holy men of the village resurrected me; they brought me back to life."

"How?"

"Rituals," he says, "ancient rites, older than Christianity. Throughout the process, the very tissues of my body were inculcated with the ability to regenerate themselves beyond death, so that I could eventually recover from any injury, no matter how horrific. And the madness that I experienced on the voyage home was the madness of death, the death of the soul, while the body endured. Can you fathom such torment?"

"Yes."

"Hmm," he says, "I believe you could at that. In any case—"

"What happened the third time?" she cuts in.

The voice chuckles, not seeming to mind the interruption; sounding perhaps amused by its impertinence. "Yes, I forget, time is growing short for you, isn't it? Well, by this point, as you may imagine, back here in America, even the most thickheaded of the yokels and hyenas who'd been hunting me down had finally gotten it through their skulls that they were dealing with something marginally more profound than a routine child slayer. Rumors had begun to circulate that I was immortal, undead, beyond death. They realized that I would persist in coming back. A kind of advocacy group formed from the parents of the children I'd taken, a vigilante army that made the previous mobs seem trivial by comparison. Counsel was sought both from the church in Boston, and up in Salem, among those practitioners of certain . . . darker faiths. One of the Salem women was Gideon Winter's older sister Sarah, whose involvement in my demise would later prove to be critical. And in time a consensus was arrived at—perhaps the first and only time in recorded history that witches and Christians have been able to agree on anything—regarding my destruction. And what do you think they decided to do?"

Sue stares through her windshield, the wind dying down, dropping the snow to offer her an absolutely clear view of the Isaac Hamilton statue coming up in front of her, the statue which no longer has arms or legs—or a head. It is simply a torso held aloft by a post, with some markings on its base.

"In 1802 they caught you and they killed you again."

"Yes . . ."

"And this time . . ."

"Yes?"

"They cut you up."

"*Yesssss.*" The voice sounds as if it's leaning toward her through the phone. There is a sickening ecstasy in it, a kind of obscene release that reminds her yet again of phone sex. "And . . . ?"

"And scattered the pieces throughout the state." She thinks of the different statues along the way, each one less than the one before it. "Your right arm, your left arm, your right and left legs, your head—" She's counting as she's saying them, mentally traveling through the towns. "Wait a minute, what about Gray Haven, with the whole statue? What's there?"

"It's just a monument of sorts. A statement of what they feared the most."

"And the last town, after your arms and legs and head?" Then she figures it out. "Your heart. The last town was where they buried your heart."

The voice on the other end says nothing. It doesn't have to.

"They cut it from your chest," Sue says, "and buried it in White's Cove. They marked each place with a monument, and they probably assigned someone to stay and watch the spot just to make sure the pieces didn't try to come back together again. And they came up with that rhyme, as a kind of charm, for extra protection. That's right, isn't it?"

The voice makes a soft, satisfied sound, smacks its lips. "Oh yes."

"But . . ." she says, and stops.

"Keep going. You're almost there."

"But it still wasn't over," Sue says, sensing the ground beneath her growing more alarmingly fragile but knowing she has to push on, because there is no more time for hesitation. The light switch is very close at hand now, intoxicatingly near, and she almost feels the tips of her fingers brushing against it. "They'd planted seeds wherever they'd buried you. Towns sprung up from each place, seven towns, founded by the statues' original guardians, and a line formed between them, connecting them. A route."

"A route," he repeats, savoring it. "Yes."

"And the curse that held your body together after you died, the spell, the magic, whatever it was . . . it spread itself out along the route, among the seven towns. That ability to resurrect dead things, dead people—it lived between the towns, along these back roads. By bringing a corpse through the towns you could restore life to it."

As she's saying this, Sue's thinking so fast that she doesn't even realize how much her head has begun to hurt. It's like the worst hangover of her life multiplied by twelve and stacked on top of a neutron bomb of a sinus headache. She thinks of Jeff Tatum and Marilyn, and how they are only hollow shells, clumsy pawns before the resurrecting power of the route. How Jeff spoke to her in the same tone, the same voice as the one on the cell phone, his human attributes swallowed and digested by the relentless black onslaught of the force that drove him: Isaac Hamilton.

"But the bodies always take on your personality. They speak with your voice. They're like empty shells. They come back not knowing they're dead until they feel you within them. Even then they might not know it—until you take over."

"That's exactly right."

Of course it is, she thinks. Dear God, how do I know all this?

Her prescience doesn't seem to bother the voice on the other end. If anything he sounds delighted that she has finally arrived at the true significance of the route and her role in it. "Very impressive, Susan.

You've come a long way tonight, both literally and figuratively. Daylight is almost in view. There's just one more thing we need to talk about."

She knows. "The Engineer."

"Yes."

"What about him?"

The voice purrs. "You tell me."

"Who was he," she asks, "really?"

"I believe I've already answered that question."

She doesn't say anything.

"Think, Susan. What I just told you."

She casts her mind back, reviewing everything he said up till now, and comes up with nothing.

Let your mind go blank. Try not to think.

She draws away, allowing her thoughts to come unfocused. Given her current psychological exhaustion, this isn't difficult. Abruptly, out of nowhere, she finds herself thinking about Gideon Winter, about the Engineer. Then she sees it.

"He was your first."

"Good, Susan."

"The very first man you killed when you came back to the States," she says, "what was his name, Gideon Winter? He was a railway engineer."

"A private joke of mine. There were no railroads then. The ironic thing is that Gideon Winter was never an 'engineer'—that was merely one of the many personas that I created for my vessel over these past two centuries."

She wants to ask him more, but senses they've

reached the point in their conversation where he will tell her what he wants. And he does.

"As I said, his older sister Sarah was one of the women from Salem," the voice says. "The one who suggested cutting my body apart and scattering it through the seven villages." Hamilton's smile is evident in his tone of voice, a thin meanness in which there is no spark of humanity. "But she couldn't let it be. She was obsessed. When she saw how the towns were sprouting up where I'd been buried, she thought about her brother, poor Gideon, lying in the cold ground. And she was seized by an idea—the notion that whatever force had animated her brother's murderer might be used to return Gideon from death itself."

"Whoever gave her that idea?" Sue says.

"Ah." He laughs. "I wish I could take credit for that, Susan. But as you no doubt have come to realize by now, I have no particular power over the living, only the dead."

"Then why did she . . . ?"

"Human nature," he says. "Unholy obsession at work in the grief-stricken mind, the same sort of morbid compulsion that drives desperate people to extreme acts every day. In that sense you might say that Sarah Winter was the true mother of the route—inadvertently, of course. And I am grateful."

Sue feels a long, cold finger trace a line down the back of her neck, between her shoulder blades. "Dear God."

"One night in midwinter of 1810, on the longest

night of the year, under cover of darkness, Sarah went back to her brother's grave, dug up his coffin, and loaded it into a carriage. She drove his body from Gray Haven, heading east down dirt roads and lumber trails to White's Cove. She wasn't quite there when she began to hear the scratching sounds coming from inside his coffin." Hamilton chuckles again, and it is the dry sound of something stirring at the bottom of a pile of dead leaves. "The last thing Sarah Winter ever saw was her brother coming out of that pine box, fully resurrected, and reaching for her throat, his eyes as black as anthracite." He pauses, letting it sink in. "But she'd already completed the trip, thus providing me with my first portal back into the world, the Engineer. He would be my emissary, my first new flesh and blood, the closest I ever had to a son. After that, there would be many, many more."

"But if that's true, the Engineer would already have to be dead in the summer of 1983, when he killed all those children."

"Of course." The voice sounds perfunctory. Not so much impatient as eager for her to get to the next step, to make the final connection. "And if we follow that line of reasoning, where does that lead us, Susan?"

"If he was already dead in 1983, and you were already controlling him, then we couldn't have really killed him in the first place."

"Of course not. You can't kill a corpse. But you did set him back in his work."

"But—"

"You *attacked* him, Susan. That's what incensed me. You attacked the one I'd come to think of as my only begotten son, brought back into the world to continue my work. I needed someone to take him through the route again, just to recover from his wounds."

"Then what's the purpose of me bringing his corpse through the route again tonight? It doesn't make sense." She's blinking, her head pounding, so close, so fucking *close* to figuring out where he's been leading her, and then it hits her all at once. "Unless . . ."

And he jumps on it. "Unless what, Susan?"

"Unless the body in the garbage bags isn't the Engineer."

She steps on the brake and the Expedition skids to a halt, the phone still clutched to her ear. Through it she thinks she can hear the voice laughing.

It doesn't even feel like she's walking anymore, or even running. It feels like she's *flying,* skimming an inch above the ground, every neuron cranked to maximum performance. She swoops around to the back, yanks open the hatch of the Expedition, and stares inside at the thing wrapped up in garbage bags. For the first time since she dug it up, she pulls the bags open and looks at the face of the thing inside.

For a fathomless span of seconds she simply stares at it, her entire body petrified by raw disbelief.

The corpse wrapped in the garbage bags—the corpse that she lugged from a slimy hole underneath the bridge, ten hours ago, and dragged halfway across

Massachusetts in the back of her SUV—is *not* wearing blue-striped overalls with a red bandanna sticking out of the pocket.

It's not the Engineer.

No, this corpse, this body, this dead human being, is dressed in a navy blue blazer and L.L. Bean khaki pants. It wears a white oxford shirt beneath the blazer, a red silk tie, with Bass loafers. It has a silver watch on its wrist and a silver wedding band on its finger.

The face and hands are pale and bruised in the places where blood has begun pooling up under the skin. It hasn't been dead for long. The decay process has only just begun. Across its face the muscles have drawn back into a tight grin, the skin of the cheeks bunching together above the teeth. Crumbs of dirt stick in the creases. There's dirt and mud in the hair as well.

And the eyes . . . the eyes are black and staring.

While she's looking at them, a shiny black beetle scurries from the corner of his mouth, trundling busily across the curved expanse of skull and ducking up into the corpse's hairline. And with that Sue vomits—no warning, no nausea, just jerks her mouth open and throws up into the snow beside the Expedition. She vomits and vomits, until there's nothing left but a bitter taste in the back of her mouth and tears in her eyes, blurring her vision to a field of soggy prisms.

But of course Sue doesn't need to see in order to

recognize the man in the garbage bags. She has seen enough for a lifetime.

"Phillip," she says, her voice stripped away to a hoarse and rasping gasp. "Oh my God."

And that's when the corpse lunges straight up at her, his swollen fingers locking around her throat.

"So you finally opened the garbage bags, you brainless little snatch."

Coming through her husband's mouth, Isaac Hamilton's voice is grating, rippled with caked filth and swamp slime. At this moment Sue realizes that the grin wrinkling across its face is not, as she first thought, the result of rigor mortis or some other half-fathomed notion of what happens to your muscles after you die. *The thing has been grinning up at her this whole time.*

She tries to twist free, but the corpse's grip is far tighter than Jeff's. And this makes sense. He's come farther along the route than Marilyn or Jeff. He's almost fully resurrected. His fingers squeeze into the soft hollow of her throat until she feels something pop, shooting a bright spike of pain through her neck.

"It fucking took you long enough," Hamilton's voice says. Crawling forward, out of the trunk, shedding the last of the tattered garbage bags, her husband's corpse jams her body up and out so that her feet are no longer touching the ground. Then he starts to shake her so hard that her legs flop and jitter, feet flying everywhere as she fights pointlessly to pry his hands off. The rotting, black-eyed face laughs at her. She fights the urge to black out, because she's certain she'll never wake up. He's going to kill her, this thing that's inside her husband, this parasite that lives in his guts.

She starts praying then, not the kind of prayer that starts *Dear God,* but the kind that goes, "From Ocean Street in Old White's Cove," spitting the words with the blood that's now pouring into her mouth. "Across the virgin land he drove—"

Phillip goes motionless, holding her upright, head tilted back. "What the fuck do you think you're doing?"

"—to paint each town and hamlet red, with the dying and the—"

Whack! He slams his head into hers so hard that she bites her tongue, incandescent waves of green stars shimmering before her eyes, the pain itself not even a factor compared to the sheer shock of the attack. When Sue hoists up her head again he's still holding her by the throat, his head angled back. "Don't you try that shit with me, you brainless, low-brow whore. It doesn't work. It's not *going* to w—"

"He walked through Wickham and Newbury," Sue says, except her tongue is bleeding and swollen and the words spill out mushy and malformed. "In Ashford or Stoneview he might tarry—"

Whack! Another blow, the corpse's skull clubbing hers like the back of a shovel, sending her reeling. *Now* the pain is here, big-time pain, an eye-popping

Las Vegas of it and then in the muffled distance, very far off, Isaac Hamilton's musty cackle.

"I'm going to enjoy this," his voice is saying behind the pain, behind the funny-colored stars and constellations that flutter close to her head, blinding her. "I'm *really* going to enjoy this, Susan."

"To call . . . child . . . to . . . knee . . ." she's mumbling, on total autopilot now, "where he slew it . . . one . . . two . . ."

WHAM! A massive blow, the worst yet, something cracking, and it pitches her whole upper body backward, the pain so intense that Sue can't help it, she feels herself start crying again, he's breaking her and she's going to let him. She's got no choice. Bright hot needles pierce her flesh from every possible angle as she feels her scalp beginning to swell with bleeding under the skin. Her mouth sags open, drooling. She can't see. She can't hear. She can only feel the pain. Unconsciousness beckons her forward as seductively as any controlled substance she can imagine and she feels herself sliding toward it gratefully, almost all the way there, when a single thought cuts through her like a bullet.

Veda.
If you black out now she's dead.
If you black out now she's dead.
If you black out now she's fucking dead.

That centers her. Blind, numb, but somehow centered, she makes her lips and tongue move. It's like a guttural foreign language that, to an uncomprehending ear, sounds more like snarling than diction, Ara-

bic or German spoken through a mouthful of stiffening rubber cement. She pushes the words out anyway
until they don't sound like any language at all. They're
merely sounds. Animal noises.

". . . un fum . . . In-sluh fuh . . . Guh *Huhn* . . .
Whuh uh *muh* . . ." It's such a completely debilitating
effort expelling these noises and she's dizzy, fading,
losing whatever's left of herself. "Whuh . . . uh . . .
muh . . ."

Far beyond the darkness that fills her eyes, through
Phillip's lips, Isaac Hamilton is laughing, laughing.
Coughing on dirt. Mimicking her feeble attempts,
mocking, "Uh-*fuh*-uh-*fuh*-uh-*fuh*—" She can hear the
stuffy noises getting more congested as his hilarity
crescendos. "I didn't know it was fucking barnyard
night, Susan. Moo, moo, cock a doodle-doo!" As he
says this, her vision clears slightly, perhaps for the
sheer novelty of seeing her husband's reanimated
corpse—a thing with maggots in its sinuses and worm
shit on its breath—making fun of her enunciation.
Through swollen eye-slits she sees Phillip's head tilting itself back again, preparing to drive forward for
the blow that will no doubt turn out her lights forever, rendering whatever good intentions she might
still have utterly irrelevant. She cringes away with the
last of her strength, and waits for it.

Then nothing happens.

"Sue . . . ?" It's so tentative, that familiar voice. It
doesn't sound like Isaac Hamilton at all. "Honey?"

Sue raises her head, manages to peel back the lid on one eye. Phillip's corpse has fallen absolutely still and is just facing her now, what's left of his face tinged pinkish. She's not sure if this coloration is due to the blood in her own eyes, or the Expedition's taillights glowing behind his head. Whatever the cause, it makes the thing look slightly more human, less dead. He's leaning over her, and that's when she realizes she's on the ground, sprawled in the snow at the side of the road, her legs tucked underneath her. When exactly did she fall down?

"Sue," he says, "is that you?"

"Phillip." His name flows from her battered windpipe in a watery whisper, zero inflection, zero strength. "Don't hit me. Don't hurt me anymore."

"Sue, honey, what's wrong, are you . . . ?" Phillip stops, and her sight is good enough now that she can see the wave of realization washing across his face, a single foamy whitecap across a midnight sea. "Oh no. Oh, Sue. Oh, baby." His legs buckle and he slumps down on the roadside next to her, the tailpipe of the

Expedition pumping exhaust out in plumes behind his head. "I'm so sorry. I don't know what to say." He holds out one hand and then lets it fall. "He's in me, Sue. I can feel him."

She nods. It hurts. Everything does.

"That's how he works."

"I don't—"

"Listen to me, Sue. Without a vessel he's only a dismembered corpse in the ground. Regardless of what he wants you to think, he can't read minds or hunt people down by himself. That's what took him so long to find me."

"Why?"

"He only has power over the corpses he commands. He had to send one of his vessels out to kill a private detective and bring him through the route just so he could get someone with the skills to locate me. I had to keep hiding. That's why I sent Tatum to warn you."

Sue's mind darts back to the farm truck following her on and off over the past few months, how it had known where to find her. "*You* sent Jeff Tatum?"

"Met him . . . at his brother Daniel's funeral in Gray Haven three years ago. Kept in touch with him after I went to California. When Hamilton started tracking me down in August, after I called the radio station, I contacted Jeff. Asked him to keep an eye on you."

"They got Tatum too," Sue says.

"I know."

"Phillip—"

"The worst part is, he never stops." Phillip's corpse

nods shakily. "Hamilton's spirit, Sue . . . it's like having a fever that won't break—you can't . . . push through it. Always there. Always building."

"How—" Sue pauses, wipes the blood from her mouth. She's pretty sure that the bleeding has begun to taper off, but the headache . . . oh, the headache is another matter. It flares up with every vibration that comes through her throat, like she's got a couple of hard cons serving time breaking granite between her eyes. She tries to focus past it, making herself look at what's left of her husband. "How did this happen?"

"Doesn't matter now."

Maybe not, but she's got a few ideas of her own. "It's because we put one of his bodies, his vessels, out of commission." Her mind swirls back to the playground, that afternoon. "His *first* one." Maybe it's the beating she just took, or the presence of Phillip's voice, or the route itself, but she can see it all clearly. "The Engineer."

"Yes," Phillip says. "You're right. Do you remember, Sue? Can you see it?"

"Yes."

And just like that, she's back in 1983.

But it's different from the way she used to recall it, in that desolate patch of abandoned playground equipment beyond the empty outskirts of her hometown. For the first time she's actually seeing it the way it happened, not the way her memory has homogenized it over the intervening years. For the first time Sue realizes why it haunted Phillip so mercilessly ever since—because he must've remembered it this way, the way it really *was*.

In the restored memory she sees the Engineer getting out of his orange Plymouth, dressed in the bib overalls with the red handkerchief dangling from the back pocket. He's wearing a big pair of aviator-style sunglasses that cover not only his eyes but also a good part of his face above the bridge of his nose. He's sporting a workman's tan, leathery and deep, and within seconds he's already moving toward them fast, like he's on roller skates or something, Sue thinking, how can any guy move so quickly—this part is still the way she's always remembered it—and the Engineer reaches behind his back, pulling out the red handkerchief, blotting at his forehead above the sunglasses.

"My goodness," he exclaims, in a just-folks voice that's somehow all the more shocking for its laconic intonation. "Sure is a scorcher out here, isn't it?"

Sue just looks at him without answering. She looks at herself reflected times two in the big lenses of his shades, a little girl with wide eyes and skinny arms.

"Boy, howdy." The Engineer jerks his head toward Phillip, standing next to her, a foot or two away. "Why, I'd think you and your friend here would be off taking a dip at the pool on a day like today, or maybe down in the creek. It's hotter than blazes out here in the sun. Enough to boil the skin right off your bones, wouldn't you say?"

"Sue, wait." Young Phillip is standing to her right,

a step or two ahead of her. He looks back at the Engineer. "You want something, mister?"

At first the man doesn't turn his head away from Sue. When he does shift his attention toward Phillip, it happens reluctantly. He blots his head with his handkerchief again, and Sue notices how gingerly he applies the square of fabric to his skin.

"You're all by yourselves out here." A sly smile seems to tease at the corners of his lips, where the skin is more than slightly cracked. "You don't get scared being out here by yourselves?"

"Scared of what?" Phillip asks, his voice trembling a little, though he does a pretty good job of holding it steady.

"Oh, I don't know. A lot could happen out here in the middle of nowhere. But I guess you can take care of yourselves, can't you? How old are you?"

"Thirteen," Sue says. It comes from her so smoothly that she almost believes it herself. Because she's tall that summer, taller than Phillip, and that helps too. She can sell this lie, she realizes; she can make him believe it. Because the Engineer never takes kids older than twelve.

"Well, I suppose I'll be on my way, then. You two kids take care." He turns around and walks back to the car, climbing in. At the last minute, he sticks his head out the open window. "Say, would you do me a favor and take a look at this map, tell me how I can get back to the interstate?"

Phillip takes another step toward the Plymouth, and then another, and Sue realizes she's going with him, because they're in for a penny, in for a pound. They started this thing by walking toward the car in the first place, and they are going to find out the truth; or at least Phillip is, which means that she is too.

Sue stops walking when she gets near the driver's side window, a safe five feet away. Behind the steering wheel, the man is holding up a map of eastern Massachusetts. He pokes a finger at a crooked line connecting a cluster of towns.

"This is where I started. . . ."

Looking up at the other side of the car, Sue sees Phillip gaping down into the Plymouth's backseat. Whatever he sees there has erased any vestige of expression from his face. Sue follows his stare. Lying there in an open cardboard box behind the driver's seat are several rolls of packaging tape, stacks of clean rags and gauze, and a large knife. The blade of the knife is very bright, very clean, and it reflects a narrow obelisk of light onto the seat cushions above it.

"I came down this way, heading west—"

In front of her, behind the wheel, the man in the bib overalls and aviator-style specs is still pointing out the route he took, tracing it with his fingertip. He doesn't appear at all concerned as Phillip wanders around the back of the Plymouth, to where Sue is standing, and stops alongside the open window of the backseat, less than a foot away from the cardboard box. She keeps waiting for the man to stop looking at the map and glance into the rearview mirror, but he doesn't.

Sue glances at Phillip, but he's looking at the knife.

No, Phillip, she thinks suddenly. This is a mistake.

"Oh, one more thing." All at once the man looks up from the map, straight at her, close enough that she can almost see through the sunglasses' tinted lenses. "I know you're lying about your age."

Sue is still processing this as Phillip grabs the knife from behind the driver's seat, comes forward between Sue and the car, and stabs the knife straight into the man's chest. The man sits straight upright, his left hand flying out in an attempt to grab the blade. And as Phillip's arm brushes against his wrist, Sue sees the fake yellowish orange color smearing off the Engineer's flesh, revealing the skin underneath to be bluish black.

Phillip swings the knife again.

His second thrust only grazes the Engineer's arm and more flesh-colored paint streaks away, sticking to the blade. But it's not just the makeup that comes off, Sue sees, it's the skin itself, peeling off the Engineer's wrist and coating Phillip's hand in a sticky smear of gristle. Phillip isn't aware of it yet, he's busy thrusting the knife back at the Engineer, shoving it hard, forcing the blade again and again into the man's chest.

And that's when the sunglasses fall off.

The eyes beneath are huge and desolate, utterly black, and they jiggle in the man's sockets like the tainted egg sacs of some unthinkable demon. Within them Sue glimpses some vestige of limited intelligence, but it's like nothing she's ever seen in the eyes of people or animals—it's completely alien, their depths animated solely by appetite which even now seems to be fading swiftly into nothingness.

Sue is still staring deep into the memory, her mind's own eye dilated to an almost perfect circle, astonished at how different things really are from the way she's recalled them in the past. She sees the Engineer's head swivel to the side, his struggles already weakening, and then suddenly his mouth opens and spurts out a spray of thick grayish black fluid across the ground. Sue sees chunks floating in the fluid, pieces of what looks like dead skin, she thinks, but there's no blood in it—and in fact, there's no blood *anywhere*. All the punctures and stab wounds across the Engineer's chest, torn to pieces, his bib overalls and thoracic cavity alike, but there's *no blood*.

And when Phillip finally stops stabbing him, he sits up, sweat trickling into his eyes, breathing in gasps, and looks at Sue. The hysteria beneath his dazed expression is rising fast, like some iridescent fish flashing just centimeters from the surface. For a second he can't speak. "What is this?" he rasps, eyes flashing down to the bloodless, black body sprawled out beneath him. "What is this, Sue? It's like—"

It's like—

"Like he's not even alive," Sue says aloud now, and realizes she's been shocked back to the present moment by the realization. "I—I blocked it out of my memory, Phillip. That whole thing, I blotted the details right out of my mind. I remembered it wrong."

"Doesn't matter," Phillip's corpse says in its flinty, rasping voice next to her.

Sue shakes her head. "It *does* matter. I always told myself we didn't tell anyone because we thought we might've gotten the wrong guy, but that's not why. We never told because we were so freaked out, and we knew no one would believe us. And eventually I never even believed us. But you remembered. You *never* forgot."

"*Doesn't matter.*" Phillip wrenches his head up toward her. "Go. Get out of here. He's coming back into me. I can feel it. Leave me here. Turn around."

"What about Veda?"

"He'll—never let her—live."

"Where is she?"

One hand flicks at her, a feeble shooing movement. "Go. Isaac Hamilton is here. Coming back into me." Urgently now, but undercut by a failing vitality. "Feel him. So close. Can't hold him back. Just . . . go."

Sue looks at him, this corpse, this cursed thing wavering in front of her and feels a single blue spark fly across her stomach and land, sizzling, in her chest, where without warning it ignites a puddle of untapped adrenaline. There's a whoosh, and she feels a wellspring of fury, a geyser of indignation and rage for which no precedent exists in her life, ever. And she says, "No."

Phillip doesn't reply. Maybe he can't. Sue throws both her arms straight out in front of her, clenching the thing by its shoulders, feeling its collarbones sticking out beneath dead skin and the fabric of the jacket. "Now you listen to me," she says. "I'm still alive. I'm not dead, and that thing doesn't own me, and until it does I'm going to fight the shit out of it. So you tell me. Where the hell is Veda?"

"Hamilton." The name like a stone. "Using her as bait. To make you bring me fully back to life. Like you said. Vengeance. For what we did that day. Attacking the Engineer. His first and favorite vessel."

"Fuck him *and* his vessel. I'm delivering you to Ocean Street as promised. And I'm getting Veda back from him."

"Sue . . . no." He's losing his voice. "A trap."

"I know it is."

"Won't be able to stop myself—from hurting you—"

"I'll handle that." She climbs to her feet, digging out infinitesimal scraps of strength from beneath the layer of fatigue and pain that was all she knew a moment ago, gathering it up and compressing it together in an airtight diamond against the wall of her heart. There's a length of tow rope in the back of the Expedition, and she grabs it. She remembers how Jeff Tatum waffled and wavered right before he started screaming at her again, and she knows she has to hit this right or else she'll have no chance at all. She waits until Phillip's face begins to twitch, the fibers contorting, hands going up to the dry sockets—

"Coming," he groans. "He's coming."

"Good," Sue says, "let him come," and in one fluid move she shoves her husband's body back into the trunk of the Expedition. Wherever Phillip is on the continuum between himself and Isaac Hamilton, the shove catches him supremely off guard because the corpse tilts and flops straight into the open space, head whacking against the hatchback before he lands inside with a thud. His legs aren't all the way in, they're sticking out at shin-level, but that's how she wants it, and she grabs the hatch and slams it down hard with both hands.

There's a dull crunch as one of the bones in his lower leg snaps, and she's not sure whether she actually hears him howl or if it's just her imagination. Not that it matters. Her hands are already moving again, looping the tow rope around the steel hitch beneath the bumper and then up to the latch-ring inside the Expedition's rear-gate, yanking the hatch down as tight as it'll go, pinning his ankles. Phillip's feet, encased in Bass loafers, squirm furiously. But they're not going anywhere.

"Let me go, you cocksucking bitch!" the thing in the back of her Expedition shrieks, back to Isaac Hamilton's voice. It's pounding on the floor, flopping around back there, gagging on rage. "I'll kill your daughter, you hear me? I'll fucking tear out her tongue! I'll rip her heart out and *eat the fucking thing*!"

"Not if I turn around and drive you straight back to Gray Haven. If I do that, you'll go back to being just another lifeless pile of skin."

"It doesn't work that way."

Sue doesn't answer, realizing he's probably right. And even if the process *is* reversible, there must be other bodies at his disposal. She thinks of the two-hundred-year period that has elapsed since Gideon Winter's sister inadvertently provided Hamilton with his first servant. One corpse could've easily driven the next through the towns, creating an entire arsenal of bodies for Hamilton to inhabit.

But maybe, she thinks, just maybe, no matter how many bodies he has to choose from, he wants Phillip's corpse in particular. And her own. Why? Because they were the only two who had ever damaged his most precious vessel, his beloved Engineer, his first infernal emissary sent back into the world to do his will.

The closest I ever had to a son.

"If you *don't* need Phillip's body," she says, "I'll turn around. Right now." She is mindful that she's walking an extremely perilous line here, gambling with lives, her own, her daughter's. But that's the only way to play it—right to the edge.

The corpse sits up and leers at her from the other side of the glass. Its legs have stopped struggling. "You wouldn't dare."

"Why not? You already told me that you're going to kill Veda. What's stopping me from sending the police into White's Cove and hauling you back to Gray Haven?" Without even waiting for an answer, she walks around to the front of the Expedition and gets behind the wheel. She puts it in drive and turns the vehicle around, arcing across both lanes so that she's facing the other way, and puts the pedal down, nose to the west, spitting snow to the east.

And that's when she hears the voice in the back say: "Wait."

"Yes?"

"All right."

She looks back at it. "What was that?"

"I said, *all right*. Bring . . ." The corpse glowers down at its own limbs, sprawled out around it. "Bring this body to Ocean Street."

"You said I had to have it there by seven thirty. There's no time."

"Never mind that. Just do it. Your daughter will be there. In exchange for bringing this body, you will get her back unharmed."

Why should I trust you now? Sue thinks, but doesn't say anything. Of course she cannot trust Isaac Hamilton any more than she ever could. But if there's a chance, however remote, that Veda is still in White's Cove then she has to go. And if things work out, if fate is kind, if she actually catches a break—

She might be able to get both of them out of there alive.

She reaches down to retrieve the map from the pile of crumpled faxes on the floor. She digs through the trash, checks under the seats, even looks in the back where her husband's body lies glowering at her.

But the map is gone.

S he finds her way east by dead reckoning.

Twice she gets completely turned around, finding herself heading down a long, open road without any landmarks, sure that she's headed in the wrong direction. At one point it gets bad enough that she starts trembling, every part of her body, and she's convinced she'll never be able to stop.

Eventually she realizes that she can smell the ocean, the first foggy tendrils of wet sand, fish, and salt that never go away no matter what season it is. Up ahead the eastern skyline has begun to lighten beneath its veil of snow, gray dawn dragging itself into the faint encrustation of starlight like old age crawling up to smother something that was once bright and beautiful. In fact, the whole landscape has a lifeless pallor to it. It feels insubstantial, weightless, monochromatic, as if the road and trees and the sloping, snow-covered hills had been sucked dry of all life during the night, leaving only their outlines, ash sculptures that might crumble and spill if she bumped into them.

In the back of the Expedition, the thing inhabiting

her husband's body doesn't speak. She can only hear it rustling around every minute or so, a sibilant restlessness of flesh and fabric that's barely loud enough to be distinguished from the hum of the tires on the road.

Out of nowhere a seagull dips across the sky, then kites upward, and her eyes follow it as the road curves to the right. Directly in front of her the gull banks sharply, rising into a part of the sky where dawn has not yet penetrated, and vanishes among what's left of the stars. Sue thinks of the sea, whose proximity is somehow more reassuring to her than the coming of daybreak. Maybe it's the way that the ocean brings the land to an end, a sense that whatever happens, there can be no more route beyond it.

There's a sign coming up and as she gets closer, Sue realizes it doesn't look like the other towns' signs. This one is bigger, the block letters carved into a slab of light, unfinished wood, pine or cedar, and mounted on massive, bare logs by the side of the road:

WELCOME TO OLD WHITE'S COVE
AN AUTHENTIC 19TH-CENTURY NEW ENGLAND VILLAGE
"TAKE A TRIP BACK IN TIME!"

As she passes the sign Sue realizes, with mild surprise, that she *has* heard of White's Cove before, the name itself so shamelessly bland that until she actually laid eyes on it, it didn't click. It's one of those communities like Plimoth Plantation or Colonial Williamsburg where the employees show up for work dressed in rigorously detailed period costumes, bonnets and buckles and waistcoats, the wooden buttons all stitched on by hand. They churn their own butter and call their children "rapscallion" and none of them are allowed to wear a digital watch on duty. The realization that this is where she's been headed all along—literally into the past—reverberates for a moment from her brain to her heart and back again like a cry in an empty street.

Off to the right, a sign with an arrow says PARKING and points to a large, empty lot surrounded by drifts of snow. Sue drives past it, realizing only afterward that the road ends here, at least the paved portion of it. The Expedition thumps onto a dirt road packed with a layer of ice, skids a bit, and then finds its way without a problem.

And without any further warning she's driving straight down Main Street, circa 1802, past barns and old mansard-roofed houses, tiny dwellings with squinty little windows and doors that seem far too small for anyone to get in or out of. The narrow street presses in on either side of the Expedition, making it feel darker than it did before she stumbled into the village. It feels colder here too, as if somebody sealed the whole thing off in a bubble and pumped in dry-ice vapor. None of the gas lamps are lit, none of the storefronts open, and Sue isn't sure if they're closed for the season or it's just too early in the morning. The dirt road in front of her is clear, though, with great mountains of plowed snow heaped up shoulder-high on either side. She cruises along looking for some kind of street sign, but maybe they didn't have them back then, though apparently they had snowplows.

The road is headed steadily downhill and she looks ahead to what's in store. Spread out below her in the beads of sea-gray dawn she can see the business part of the village leading into the square, and the wharf beyond it. This is no doubt the home of the requisite smithy and baker and butter churn and the wooden stockade where the kids can get their pictures taken with head and hands through the restraints.

To the right and left she can see several other roads coming down to converge at the low point like spokes on a wheel, and at the axis of the wheel—scarcely visible from here—is a dark statue standing atop a stone pillar.

Three guesses what that is.

Seeing it, she knows it doesn't matter whether she finds Ocean Street or not, because this is where she's going to be meeting the Engineer, where Isaac Hamilton will—or won't—trade Veda for the body of Phillip. This really is the end of the line.

Because this is where he kills you, *so he can take* your *body back to Gray Haven. This is where he gets what he's really after.*

Behind her back, the thing wearing Phillip's skin starts laughing.

It is a revolting sound, chunky and clotted, like someone choking on thick chowder. The laugh keeps escalating in volume and intensity. Sue is about ready to put the Expedition in park and just get out, *any-*

thing is better than listening to that laugh, when straight ahead of her in the middle of the road, she sees something half-buried in a pile of snow.

There's a shovel sticking out of the pile, as if someone was in the middle of burying it when she happened to come by. Then the wind picks up, a sharp gust that blasts the top layer of snow away, and Sue sees what it is.

It's a large wicker basket, the size of a washtub. And it's right there, so close, well inside her headlights but engulfed in snow. If she hadn't stopped when she did, she might have run it right over.

She opens the door and jumps down, reaching the basket in three steps, and yanks the lid off. Inside, staring straight up at her, looking very small and very still, is the body of her daughter.

Veda isn't crying.
Veda isn't moving.
Veda is blue.

Sue clasps the lifeless form in her arms, holding her to her chest, rocking her in her arms. The discolored skin of her daughter's face feels as cold as museum marble, hardly yielding to Sue's touch. The eyes continue to stare, endlessly.

Leaving Sue to think: No. This can't be right. Not when I've come this far. You can take everything. Just not this. Never this. The thoughts aren't conscious thoughts, just fragments, and she croons to her daughter, supporting Veda's head, singing the first song that comes to mind, "The Itsy-Bitsy Spider."

"The itsy-bitsy spider went up the water spout. . . ." Behind her she hears a steel latch clank and she's dimly aware of the thing climbing out of the back of the Expedition, freeing itself now that the ride is over. And she knows now that it's *always* been able to free itself, that the façade of hope has always been nothing more than that, just another façade. Another joke to get her here.

"Down came the rain and washed the spider out. . . ." Sue Young lies down in the snow with her daughter cradled in her arms. The snow doesn't feel cold. It doesn't feel like much of anything. It could easily be her grave, and maybe it will be before long, what difference does it make? "Out came the sun and dried up all the rain." Sue's eyes are dry, and they fasten on to her daughter's; she doesn't want to look at anything else, ever again. "And the itsy-bitsy spider went up the spout again. . . ."

So much stillness, all around.

"I love you," she whispers. "I love you, Veda."

Then as the snow pushes against her, she feels a mild twitch against her chest, Veda curling toward her. And in that second Sue stops breathing. Her breath is . . . gone. Her daughter lifts her head and looks at Sue, recognition flooding her eyes. As Sue looks back at her, Veda draws in a deep breath; her mouth opens in a wide, dark oval and she begins to cry.

"Oh honey" is all Sue gets out, as she bursts into tears with her. Veda clutches her tighter, burying her head in Sue's neck, and Sue feels so much weight, sheer metric tonnage levitating from her shoulders that for a moment she's sure that she can lift right off the skin of this miserable planet and leave it all behind. Just her and her daughter, floating.

Please be true. Please don't be another trick.

Even as she thinks this, hugging her daughter, kissing Veda's head and holding her, Sue is terribly sure that a trick is *exactly* what it is. At the moment it's much easier to fear the worst than hope for the best. What if something happened to Veda, what if those—things did something to her? What if her little girl is really dead and this is some unspeakable, route-resurrected version of her daughter, the killing blow to sanity?

But as Veda howls and digs her fingers into Sue's sweatshirt, her face turning pink again, Sue begins to think otherwise. Except for the possible hypothermia from lying in the basket, Veda doesn't appear to be hurt, and her behavior is exactly as Sue remembers. She's just—she's her *daughter*, that's all, and this morning there is a God who has been watching out for both of them throughout this unthinkably cruel errand.

Sue, thinking these things as she calms her daughter, promising her that it's over and everything will be all right, sees the front door of one of the little houses open up, and Marilyn and Jeff Tatum shamble out into the snow. They both have those large, shimmering black eyes now, not so much the eyes of a shark, as Sue thought before, but more like a giant squid, great and round and moist. Covered in blood, the two corpses swivel and start moving toward her. They speak as one, in the same voice.

"I *always* keep my promises, Susan."

Sue turns and starts back toward the Expedition. A few feet beyond it she can see Phillip's corpse standing there, head cocked in her direction, not moving.

She swings the door open and puts Veda in back, as far as possible from the broken passenger window. Sue jumps in behind her, stretching over the backseat to slam the hatch down before hitting the locks.

They are outside, looking in at her. *Three of them, plus the Engineer, wherever he is.* She scans the street, down to the square, and picks up the cell phone, dialing 911. *I've got my daughter back now, you bastard, and there's nothing in the world that's going to stop me from calling in every cop from here to Springfield.*

The 911 operator picks up on the second ring. "Nine-one-one, police services, what is the nature of your emergency?"

"I'm being attacked," Sue says, her voice steady. Next to her, Veda has stopped crying and sits watching her with the gimlet-eyed fascination that children bring to the moments when they somehow know that everything's at stake. "My daughter and I are in White's Cove, and we're inside a blue Ford Expedition. There are at least three—"

Three *what*? She pauses, struggling with the words, looking out at Jeff and Marilyn and into the rearview at Phillip, their black eyes fixed on her.

". . . assailants right outside my vehicle. We can't get out."

"We'll dispatch a unit immediately," the operator says. "What did you say your location was?"

"White's Cove."

"Excuse me?"

"White's Cove. It's north of Boston. It's the old historic village. It's north of Boston," she says again. "Just look on a map, for God's sake, you can't miss it."

"Do you know the name of the street you're on?"

"I can't—there are no street signs that I can see, it's just—" Sue stares out the window. Jeff and Marilyn have started to move again, walking steadily toward her. She checks the mirror. Phillip isn't there. She doesn't see him anywhere. Next to her Veda is staring through the windshield, making fast, urgent sounds, pointing at Marilyn. "Min!" she cries. *"Min! Min!"* She thrusts her hand at Marilyn excitedly, recognizing her nanny despite the fact that Marilyn's eyes are gleaming black and the front of her shirt is layered in blood.

Marilyn and Jeff are only ten feet in front of her now, clutching each other as if sharing in some private joke. They come closer. Sue reaches over and pulls Veda's seat belt over her small shoulder, then puts the Expedition into drive.

"Ma'am?" the operator is asking. "Are you still there? You need to tell us where you are, any sort of physical description of the streets, the—"

"White's Cove—center of town. Just send someone." Sue floors the gas. The Expedition shoots forward, ramming Marilyn and plowing Jeff underneath its front tires. Marilyn's body flops up onto the hood, her face plastered against the glass just inches from Sue's own, her squid-eyes swimming, mouth still grinning as her cheek smears sideways on a streak of blood. Veda stops saying *Min!* and sits straight upright, blinking, speechless, in shock.

"Don't look, sweetie." Sue hits the brakes, throws it into reverse, and whips backward, Marilyn sliding off the hood. There's a crunch that she assumes is Jeff, then the Expedition gets stuck and doesn't go any farther. Sue puts it in drive, reverse, and then drive again, but she's high-centered on one of the drifts at the top of the street, the wheels gouging out snow until they're screaming off of nothing. She feels the Expedition tilting, the nose angling into gravity, suspended here on a single lump of snow beneath the undercarriage.

In front of her another door on one of the small, old-fashioned houses opens, and Sue sees something coming out—a smaller shape, its form so mangled, so badly decayed that at first she doesn't even recognize it as human.

But it is, or it was—a child.

And behind it, another.

Sue tries to swallow, finds no moisture in her throat and coughs. Her eyes flick to the sideview mirror. Behind her, all around her, children fill the street. They spill in stumbling profusion, their black eyes like holes punched through the very texture of time itself. Moving on the Expedition in a teeming mass.

Detective Yates, from the corner of her mind: *They dug up her body, took it away. They did it with all of them.*

Sue stares at the children. *His* children. From the summer of 1983, and 1793, and all the summers in between, and all the summers since. Their faces black with the rage of the dead. More than she can count.

Surrounding the vehicle, filling every window, approaching the glass. Fingers scratch against it, peeling at the rubber gaskets with horrible eagerness.

The cell phone begins to ring. She doesn't answer it.

She doesn't have to. Outside she can already hear Isaac Hamilton, laughing.

The children crawl up on the hood and begin pounding the windshield with their fists. Sue pulls Veda from the passenger seat, squeezes into the back, and sees them through the rear window. They're on top of the Expedition too—she hears them up there scurrying over the roof in quick furtive movements, like rats, and sees one peering down from above at her, dragging the cold ice of its bare-bone fingertips against the glass. Veda looks at the face, her eyes going wide, the corners of her mouth melting downward as two large, frightened tears roll down her cheeks.

"It's all right, baby."

Is it? I don't think so. I don't think you can get much further from "all right" than this. And if you don't come up with something right now—

Sue's gaze darts over the interior of the Expedition and settles on the box in the back, an idea forming in her mind. She parks Veda in the backseat, dead center, as far from the windows as possible, and buckles her in. "Stay here." Veda just cries harder, arms outstretched, needing to be consoled, but Sue can't be with her right now. "Baby, it's okay, we're almost done."

Kneeling next to her daughter, Sue sticks her arm into the back, rips open the cardboard case, and pulls out two bottles of the liquor she's been riding with all night. In the midst of everything, the label catches her eye. It's 151-proof rum, she realizes—her reward for getting Sean Flaherty his little piece of real estate on 151 Exeter Street.

Thank you, Sean.

She tosses both bottles into the front seat, then grabs two more, crawls back into the front, and peels off the plastic seals, uncapping each one. Fumes of high-proof alcohol immediately begin to flood the car as she grabs a handful of the wadded-up faxes from the floor. She twists up the papers, ramming them down the necks of the bottles, spilling some of the rum on another piece as she punches the dashboard lighter.

Next to her, behind her head, she hears glass shatter. She feels a small, cold hand groping in the roots of her hair, and ignores it. The cigarette lighter pops out and Sue jerks it free at the same moment that she hears Veda's crying becoming one long scream.

Sue's head snaps around and she sees them crawling in through the back windows, the dead children, coming at her daughter from both sides. They're using one another to stand on, holding one another up, one of them already head-and-shoulders into the backseat.

"Leave her alone," Sue snarls, and touches the lighter's red-hot tip to the rum-soaked fax paper in her left hand. It goes up with a sudden *whoomph* of heat and light and Sue waves the burning paper at the children clustering in the windows. They don't pull away from it, but they don't come forward either— for a second they just hang where they are, half in and half out, waiting to see what's going to happen next. She drops the lighter on the floor, touching the burning sheets to the pages she's wadded up in the liquor bottles, then uncaps another bottle and splashes as much booze as she can on the children trying to attack her daughter. Veda is screaming, arms outstretched, begging Sue to take her away from this.

Almost there, honey. Just one more second.

And Sue heaves the burning wad at the corpse on the right. There's a loud pop and the thing is immediately enveloped in a thin jacket of flame, flailing, struggling to retract itself from the car. Black smoke billows off of it along with a high, sick stench that defies metaphor. Within seconds the backseat of the vehicle has started to burn.

Sue lunges forward, unbuckles Veda, and pulls her out of the seat—Veda practically leaping into her arms—and picks up the two remaining paper-stuffed bottles with her free hand. They're heavy and slick with spilled alcohol, and one of the bottles slides out, bounces, and hits the floorboards, the clear liquor glugging out under the seat. Sue tucks the other one under her arm, cradles Veda, and swings herself out of the burning vehicle.

The children crowd before her, a wall of stolen flesh. Beyond them the street slopes downward toward the last statue at the bottom of the hill.

Sue looks at the remaining bottle in her hand, then at the mound of snow with the shovel next to it, where Veda was half-buried in her basket. She leans back, touching the fax-paper fuse to the flames flickering from inside the Expedition. The instant she sees the paper ignite, Sue hurls the bottle dead-center into the army of murdered children, whipping her body around 180 degrees in the same motion, arms and shoulders curling to protect Veda.

The force of the explosion hits her like a battering ram, pushing her away on a wave of heat so intense she feels her skin baking dry. She and her daughter both collapse into the wonderful coolness of the snow. When she sits up, clutching Veda with both hands, Sue sees the corpses churning in a sea of fire, scrambling everywhere at once. The air is filled with an awful screaming noise, of pain and fury, and the acrid odor is everywhere. And as bad as the stench is, the noise is worse. It's the sound of Isaac Hamilton screaming from every mouth.

Sue doesn't wait.

She already knows that she'll get only one chance at this, maybe not even that. Running with Veda down the long slope of the hill, she shifts her daughter's weight to her left side and grabs the shovel sticking out of the snow, not slowing down. Fifteen feet later she loses her footing and lands flat on her ass, sliding and scrambling with the shovel in one hand and Veda in the other. Sue manages to slow herself, uses the shovel to get up again, and keeps running on the edges of her feet. Three-quarters of the way down she snaps a glance back over her shoulder.

Up at the top of the street, the children are still milling around the burning Expedition—some of them are on fire but not many, most are getting reorganized, pulling themselves together. Sue doesn't know how much time she has. In the end she supposes it doesn't matter.

Moving again, she finally gets down to the bottom where the different roads converge along the town's little mock waterfront. Directly in front of her, the last statue is situated in a wide circle of black dirt, rising ten feet over her head. It is simply a stone pillar, maybe sixteen inches in diameter, with a large metal object mounted on top. Sue doesn't have to look any closer to know that the sculpted object is an oversized model of a human heart. Isaac Hamilton's heart. This is where they buried the last of him, that monster, that history of murder in New England, at the end of the route.

She steps into the circle of dirt and feels it trembling under her feet, rhythmically, thump-*thump,* thump-*thump*. The ground is shaking hard enough to make the pillar tremble visibly, and she can see the statue of the heart on top shaking along with it. It starts pounding harder, and on some level Sue knows this is because Hamilton's heart is pumping its will, its fury, into every corpse at its disposal.

She puts Veda down—the girl shrieking in terror as

soon as Sue lets her go—and plunges the shovel into the dirt. But the frozen top layer of the ground is as hard as asphalt, and the blade of the shovel bounces off it, the plastic handle vibrating in Sue's palms. Below her Veda immediately grabs Sue's leg and tries to climb up into her arms. Holding her daughter back with her left leg, Sue puts the blade down again and drives it with her right foot.

This time the blade does go in a few inches, the crust of the earth yielding to the force of her attack. She can feel the heart beneath her feet laboring harder with each pulse, wiggling through the shovel's handle and through her palms, and when she looks up again she sees that the children have turned back from the Expedition and are headed down the hill toward her.

Sue thrusts harder, slamming the shovel in, digging up as much as she can and pulling it out again. She starts to sweat and her bangs stick to her forehead. Veda clings to her leg and screams, and Sue tries to put the screams out of her mind. The ground beneath them pulses. The hole at the base of the statue has become a shallow trench, going a foot or two down at its deepest part. As she stares into it, the trench vibrates faster, making crumbs of dirt slide back down.

It's here. I know it is. I can feel it.

When she looks up, Sue sees that the children have surrounded her again. But this time they have stopped, ten paces away, coming no closer. She doesn't question it, just keeps digging, picking the shovel blade up and ramming it down.

Not deep enough.

She plunges it harder, pulls it out, smashes it in again, and the shovel clanks off something solid.

Sue looks in at it, the outer edge of what seems to be an ancient metal box. The box is shaking so hard, pulsating, that the ground around it gapes open visibly with every beat. It looks as if it's going to shake itself loose from the half-frozen ground and burst open any second and Isaac Hamilton's heart will come flying straight out at her.

If I can just get it out, get it out—

She digs the shovel in, putting all her strength into working the edge of the blade under the box, trying to get enough leverage to pry it up. It skips and scrapes off the edge.

"Come on," she says under her breath. "Come on, now. You can do this."

And drives the shovel down, one last time, sinking the blade underneath, forcing the handle up in combination with the box's own shaking, tearing up out of the earth.

Sue hunches over, reaches for the box, curling her fingers beneath its lower edges, and lifts it all the way out of the ground. She can feel it pulsating in her hands, making her arms shake along with it.

What now? What the fuck now?

Behind her there's a soft click of a bolt-action being snapped into place. Sue lowers the metal box and looks back at what the children have been looking at, in their dead and staring way, for the last moment or so.

The Engineer stands on the other side of the statue

with his rifle, the flesh of his face stretched into a tight grin. He's holding a cell phone in his right hand, the phone, she knows, that he's been calling her on all night. Sue sees how his overalls are still slashed to pieces where Phillip drove the knife in over and over, all those years ago. Next to him, Phillip's corpse is holding a long knife in front of his face, also grinning. Together they represent the leering face of Isaac Hamilton.

"Thought we'd give you the choice, Susan," Hamilton's voice says through the Engineer's mouth.

"One for you, the other for your daughter," the voice says through Phillip's mouth. It sounds identical to the other voice, the voice on the phone, the voice of Jeff Tatum and Marilyn. It is the last voice that so many children heard over the past two hundred years. "Maybe we should use the knife on the little girl."

Sue moves to pull Veda closer to her, keeping the pounding, vibrating metal box against her side with her other hand. She can hardly hold on to it. "I don't think so," she says.

"What?"

"Not as long as I've got your heart in my hands."

The Engineer shakes his head. "My heart has been locked up for centuries. You can't harm it any more than you can save yourself." He aims the rifle at her face, directly at her eyes. "Hold very still now. You'll be joining us shortly."

"All right." With her right arm Sue lifts Veda up so that the girl's face is next to hers, then raises the shaking box upward so that it's directly in front of them, blocking their eyes. She can actually hear the sound of the heart inside now, pounding the metal interior, an accelerated WHUMP-*WHUMP*, WHUMP-*WHUMP*, WHUMP-*WHUMP*. "Fire away."

Don't be stupid. He'll just shoot your legs out. It's over. You know it is.

Sue casts her glance back up the hill, over the congregation of silent children, where the Expedition is on fire. She thinks of the 151 in the trunk and the remaining half-tank of gas.

The Engineer, Phillip, and all the children stare at her, then as one they lift their gazes up the hill to where the mound of snow that had been holding the Expedition in place has melted away in the fire. And as Sue watches, the Expedition shifts free, its exhaust system scraping off whatever's left of the snow beneath it, and begins to roll downhill, flames dancing in its windows, speeding over the shaking ground, a taxi dispatched from the depths of hell.

WHUMP-*WHUMP*, WHUMP-*WHUMP*, WHUMP-*WHUMP*—

The children have turned completely around to look—the Expedition is now just fifty feet away, now forty, thirty—and as the Engineer and Phillip start to shift away, Sue tucks the metal box under her left elbow, clutching Veda against her right side, and takes three steps from the base of the statue. On the third step she launches herself as hard as she can, putting everything she has and a little more into her legs. At the same time she swings her arm backward, flinging the box directly into the path of the Expedition.

What happens next transpires as much in her mind's eye as it does in reality. The box strikes the last Isaac Hamilton statue and starts to bounce forward just as the car hits the foundation. In the last flickering instant before impact, Sue sees a brief flash of the box as it disappears between the Expedition's front grille and the statue's base, the top bursting open, its metal dimensions suddenly crushed as unstoppable force meets immovable object, and the black heart within it smashed flat, pulverized between the two.

She looks away.

Somewhere behind her Sue hears the final moments of the collision, imagines what's left of the entire crate of 151 flying forward to slam into the burning backseat. Alcohol igniting, bottles bursting like bombshells inside the Expedition, until with one shrill, ear-ringing blast, the gas tank finally explodes, shooting a tower of orange flame and black smoke straight up into the sky.

Sue raises her head, her hands pressed over Veda's ears as she looks back at the street behind her. The smoke is too thick to see through. It burns her eyes, siphons through her lungs, makes her choke. Lifting Veda up, she carries her away, down toward the waterfront. Somewhere between the street and the harbor she realizes that the sound of the pounding heart has stopped.

They get to the water, the wooden boardwalk leading to a series of docks. The air is clearer here and Sue holds Veda at eye level, the girl no longer screaming, just crying steadily, the intensity of her panic having drained her.

Sue hugs her daughter tightly, as tightly as she dares, kissing away her tears. "Shhh, it's okay," she says. Over Veda's shoulder, Sue can see the smoke rising, catching in the wind and being pulled eastward, out to sea.

And as the air slowly clears, she sees the statue is still there atop its stone pillar, the front end of the wrecked Expedition wrapped around it, burning.

Sue looks out at the hillside leading down to the water. Through the dissipating smoke she glimpses the streets, the little houses and narrow storefronts of White's Cove, and eventually she can see the bodies of the children, so many children, sprawled motionless in the snow.

She turns her daughter's head away.

Down by the water, a burning scrap of paper blows across her feet, caught in the wind. Holding Veda close to her chest, Sue leans over and lifts it by the edge that isn't on fire.

It's the map, or what's left of it. She's not sure how it got here, but in light of last night's events, the map's sudden reappearance doesn't seem the least bit surprising or strange. As charred as it is, Sue can barely make out some of the names of the towns. The first odd thing she notices is that there is no more jagged line running across it. She finds Gray Haven and tries to follow the route east but can't find the next town. At the moment she can't even remember what it was called. As the flame inches upward toward the top of the map the town names are consumed one by one, and she doesn't see any that sound like they were on the route. Now she's squinting at it, and as she does, the last of the names—White's Cove—also disappears, just a second or two before the nearby towns that surround it. Spectral images fading along with the memory of the route, vanishing down the pipeline of the night.

The route created the towns, she thinks. They're still here but the route is gone.

Up at the top of the hill she sees the lights of emergency vehicles flashing red and blue against the steadily illuminating sky.

ONE YEAR LATER

The Grand Wailea Resort rises up on Maui's south shore, a gleaming oasis in a muscular row of similar high-end hotels, though the Wailea is obviously the official winter palace of the American ruling class. From her balcony, overlooking the palms and the big bright blueberry colada of the Pacific, Sue Young can just barely make out the volcano rising on the northeastern part of the island. Much closer is the resort's own volcano, this one made of chicken wire and plaster, with its own gushing renal system of waterslides twirling down the sides into a network of interconnecting tunnels, manufactured river currents, and grotto bars. The air smells like cocoa butter and sea salt, alive with the sounds of children's feet spanking the cement around the pool as their parents sit nursing whiskey hangovers with blender drinks and a side of pineapple. In this flyspeck of the world, Sue has discovered, even your fifteen-minute oil change comes with a pineapple wedge.

Far beyond the palm trees and the private beach, where the ocean goes from pale blue to a deeper green,

Sue can see a pelican chasing its shadow across the surface, skimming low enough that the tips of its wings leave little Vs in the water. Tonight there will be whales breaching in the middle distance, their tails clearly visible from shore. She and Veda watched them last night, rising and then vanishing massively against the setting sun. She studies the pelican for some uncertain span of time, and then turns back to the suite, where Veda lies in bed, her blanket tucked in her mouth, deep in the throes of her afternoon nap.

One year, Sue thinks, gazing at her daughter. One year to the day. My God.

She looks at the unopened bottle of vodka brought up by room service, only an hour before. After years of sobriety, she's not particularly surprised to find herself craving liquor again. The pills they give her don't work and she doesn't like the lingering numbness in her neck and shoulders as they wear off, so alcohol it shall be. No doubt the results will be as dreary as they are predictable, but these days—most days—she can't find it in herself to care.

She looks out the window again. The pelican is gone.

The last twelve months have been the longest of her life, as if that endless night one year ago has done permanent damage to her sense of temporal perception, stretching the minutes and hours until they become transparent, meaningless. Certainly there has been enough collateral damage, psychological and otherwise, though it's hard to count the cost in any kind of physical way. Even with a year's perspective, all Sue knows is that certain infinitesimal mental faculties, her ability to make the smallest decisions—like whether to get out of bed in the morning—seem to have been dealt a crippling blow.

At first it was easy: There *were* no decisions to be made—only regiments of lawyers, cops, officials, men and women in suits and uniforms whisking her from one room to another, patiently asking her questions, questions, questions. There were tape recorders and cameras and polygraphs, locked rooms and white walls and clean, polished tables. Most of the people at that phase were civil enough, but even in her post-traumatic state Sue recognized that the veneer of friendship masked a stunned incredulity, a horror so vast and uncomprehending that they themselves could barely contend with it.

AREA WOMAN FOUND AMID DOZENS OF CHILDREN'S BODIES, the papers had trumpeted.

MYSTERIOUS MASS GRAVE MATERIALIZES NORTH OF BOSTON.

BOSTON WOMAN: "THE DEAD ABDUCTED MY DAUGHTER."

GRAY HAVEN MYSTERY DEEPENS AS INVESTIGATION CONTINUES.

As the story leaked and then gushed its way all over the world, the media had reacted accordingly to her story of the night before—of what she'd told them about Isaac Hamilton and the Engineer and the towns and the route that connected them—with universal revulsion and disdain. There had been panels and committee meetings and more judges and lawyers than Sue had ever thought existed, and even now her own attorney, the steadfast David Feldman, is doing his damnedest to keep the state from taking Veda away from her. As far as Sue understands it, the only thing keeping her from a psych ward or prison is the fact that nobody could actually prove that she killed anyone. Yet her story—repeated endlessly, in an unwavering litany of the facts as they'd seared themselves into her skull that night—continues to infuriate legions of local, state, and federal law enforcement officials, who insist, at the very least, that Sue Young be committed to an institution for long-term psychiatric care.

"They can't make it stick, Sue," David told her in their last conversation, a week ago. "There are still too many things that have gone unexplained, too much that they can't pin on you. That may change tomorrow, or the next day—this is going to go on for a long, long time—but in the meantime you need to do whatever you can for you and Veda."

David, Sue wanted to ask but didn't, *what do you think really happened that night? Do you believe me? Do you believe me at all?*

Better not to ask; better not to know. In actuality Sue does have some small clue about whether or not he believes her, but the truth is, she doesn't want to think about that now.

And so here she is, exactly one year later, half a world away, seeking solace in the fabled blue depths of the Pacific. Sue is staring at her daughter, breathing deeply in the center of the queen-size bed they've shared since arriving on the island Sunday.

She reaches for the vodka bottle and the water glass on the room service tray, unscrews the bottle's cap, and pours herself three fingers, bringing it to her lips. She can almost taste the sting of the alcohol when, from the corner of her eye, she sees Veda roll over in bed, still clutching her blanket tightly to her chest. Veda's lips move, and Sue recognizes the word "Mama," whispered clearly enough. The little girl's arms go out from the depths of sleep, grasping for a parent who isn't there.

Sue puts the glass down without drinking from it and gets on the bed. Lying down next to Veda, she pulls her daughter close and kisses her sleeping, dreaming eyelids. The girl stirs but doesn't awaken. Sue has no doubt that someday in the future, she will have to tell her daughter what happened that night, and there will be consequences . . . for there are always consequences when the truth comes out, and sometimes the truth costs you everything.

But that day is not today, nor tomorrow, nor will it be next week or next month or next year. For now, regardless of whatever else happens, Sue Young is going to hold her daughter in her arms and offer up a prayer (yes, a prayer, and any ambulance driver who tells you they don't pray is either lying or heartless, or both) of humbled thanks, to whatever god may be listening.

"We made it, baby," she whispers in her daughter's ear, not loud enough to wake her. She's crying now, a single tear running over the bridge of her nose. "We're home."

Yet even as she lies here with tears in her eyes, she cannot help but think again of David Feldman's comment to her a week ago, just before she left Boston, the only remark he's made to her that indicated he might actually believe she's telling the truth.

There's one thing that's been bothering me for a while, Sue. This metal box by the statue that was supposed to contain Hamilton's heart. You said you saw it crushed between the Expedition and the stone base of the statue. You know they sorted this smashed box out of the wreckage? But they supposedly couldn't find evidence of anything in there. It was empty.

Sue looks over at the clock on the nightstand. It is two thirty in the afternoon, Hawaii-Aleutian Time; in New England it is well past dusk on the longest night of the year.

It was empty.

"No," she says, the word escaping her in a whisper. "It's nothing."

But she closes her eyes and thinks again of what Phillip told her, so long ago, how the past is never done with you, not in any substantial way. How its bloody fingerprints will never come off. Not now. Not ever. A sudden coolness spreads through the hotel room, as if the warm equatorial sun has disappeared behind a cloud.

And next to her, on the nightstand, the phone begins to ring.

Read on for an excerpt from
Joe Schreiber's terrifying new thriller,

EAT THE DARK

Published by Del Rey Books
Available at bookstores everywhere

Mike Hughes thought: *It's dead.*

From where he stood, Tanglewood Memorial Hospital rose like a pile of bones, the remains of some animal that had fallen down behind the acres of trees that surrounded it and never gotten up.

On the other side of the rotunda, he saw workmen on scaffolding and ladders, hammering sheets of plywood across the windows, filling the evening air with the reassuring tap-tap-tap of endless American labor. They'd been working all week, covering every door and window to dissuade any thieves or vandals who would soon be tempted by Tanglewood's unwatched grounds, and now the work was virtually complete. The entire building was boarded shut in an irregular crossword puzzle of wooden planks.

In two hours it would be dark. It was the Fourth of July weekend, temperatures in the mid-nineties with the kind of humidity that gave even the lightest fabrics an itchy, clutching dampness. Mike continued along the walkway, the moist heat creating little sweat-blotches on the front of his blue scrub pants, and stopped outside the main entrance, where two men in yellow hard hats were packing up the last of their tools and carrying them to a waiting pickup.

"Almost done?" Mike asked.

"Just about," one of the men said, not bothering to look up.

"How are people getting through?"

The hard hat nodded vaguely off to the right. "Emergency room exit."

Mike followed the cement path beneath the long overhang where decades of ambulances had dropped off decades of casualties. Exchanging sun for shadow, his eyes lost their squint and his face softened, becoming younger, friendlier. He was thirty-four years old, an age that had once seemed as insurmountable as Everest but now felt as lived-in as his old beach sandals. Parenthood had added the first wrinkles around his eyes, and his hairline was beginning to thin. Lately, without saying anything about it, Sarah had begun buying low-fat snacks and sending salads with his supper, which he knew was as close as she'd ever come to remarking on the fact that they were both, unthinkable as it once seemed, broaching the hinterlands of middle age.

Mike went inside, walking past Steve Calhoun in his alcove set just within the emergency room entrance.

"Seven o'clock already?" Calhoun asked, scowling down at the Sports page.

"Almost."

"Ain't you the eager beaver." The security guard

shook his head. "My old man said never trust a fella that isn't late for work once in a while."

"Sounds like the model employee."

"Then there's you," Calhoun continued on, "never been a minute late in your life. Coming in early, even." He seemed to mull it over in his mind. "Man like that must have something real special waiting for him downstairs."

"Excuse me?"

"Come on, sweet Jolie Braun?"

Mike flushed. "Now listen— "

"Okay, take it easy," Calhoun said, looking up from his newspaper to nod at the wall of video monitors rising alongside him. "I get paid to notice things, that's all. Doesn't mean I got to tell nobody." A smile crept over his face. "You're a married man, ain'tcha? Got a kid at home?"

Mike set his hands on the security counter and leaned forward, forcing Calhoun to meet his eyes. "You're way off base on this."

"Not that I blame you. Lord knows I'd give my left one to get my hands around some of that."

"Look—"

"All right, all right, don't get all bent out of shape." Calhoun leaned back on his rickety stool and Mike heard the big key ring on his belt jingle. "You know, I'm surprised they even made your sorry ass come in to work tonight. You must have really pissed somebody off up the food chain, huh?"

Mike blew out his breath, relieved at the turn in conversation. "Must have."

"And the midnight shift no less?" Calhoun scowled at him, the incredulity building in his eyes like an impending sneeze. "Christ Jesus, there ain't even anybody here! Ambulance fleet transferred the last patients out to Good Sam's this morning. All that's left is files and furniture. Otherwise this whole place is as hollowed-out as my checking account."

"Suits me." He watched Calhoun's hand move automatically to the breast pocket of his uniform, finding the soft-pack of discount cigarettes, shaking one out and installing it expertly between his lips. Though he couldn't have been much older than Mike, Calhoun's entire physical appearance betrayed a lifetime of spectacular misuse and neglect. He was a scrawny, limping, unshaven man with an enormous Adam's apple who nonetheless evoked a kind of brute durability, as if the very ligature of his body was strung together by alcohol-cured leather.

For the three years Mike had worked at Tanglewood, Calhoun's "office" had been a gauntlet that he had to run just to get to the time clock. Here the security guard sat with his keys, cigarettes, and closed-circuit video feeds from every corner of the hospital, as protected as any endangered species: the gainfully employed American functional alcoholic. And from the current smell of things, Calhoun hadn't waited until he was home to start drinking.

Let him say what he wants about Jolie Braun, Mike decided. Nobody would believe him anyway.

"Ayuh." Calhoun grinned in a way that made his long chin appear to grow even longer. "I guess you ought to have it quiet tonight." He looked around with the comical bewilderment of the person the universe had chosen as its straight man more often than not. "But I still don't see why they couldn't give you one night off."

"I appreciate your concern." Mike was already leaning into the first step that would carry him away from Calhoun and whatever remained of this conversation when he heard rubber squealing up the service road in front of the hospital. Turning, he saw a line of police cruisers pulling into the rotunda, followed by an ambulance. Officers in blue uniforms were already getting out, moving with the swift urgency of men about their work.

Calhoun glanced up. "What the hell is all this happy crap?"

"Got your patient here," a young cop in sunglasses said, walking up, thrusting a fat stack of pages in Calhoun's direction.

"Hold it." Calhoun put down his paper and stood up. But the EMTs were already opening the back of the ambulance, unloading a stretcher with a man in an orange prison jumpsuit strapped to the rails. The man stared into the blue summer sky with an absolute vacancy of expression that seemed to Mike's eye neither childlike nor tranquil. Like the hospital, he thought, the man on the stretcher looked dead.

"Says here he's going for an MRI," the sunglasses cop said. "Either you two geniuses know where that is?"

Mike nodded. "I work there."

"Yeah? Well, that makes you my new best friend."

Craning his neck, Mike tried to get a better look at the face of the man strapped to the litter, but the shadows of the officers surrounding him continued to float over his features, obscuring them like a series of ill-fitting masks. It felt like the man's face was hiding from him, ducking away just when he thought he might catch a glimpse of it. The cops, all five of them, stood looking at each other across the stretcher. Mike realized that the paramedics had already climbed back into the ambulance; within moments the vehicle sped off, leaving them there with the silent passenger.

"Who is this guy?" Mike asked.

Nobody said a word.